Anne Perry is a *New York Times* bestselling author noted for her memorable characters, historical accuracy and exploration of social and ethical issues. Her two series, one featuring Inspector Thomas Pitt and one featuring Inspector William Monk, have been published in multiple languages. Anne Perry was selected by *The Times* as one of the twentieth century's '100 Masters of Crime' and now lives in Scotland.

Praise for Anne Perry:

'A complex plot supported by superb storytelling'

Scotland on Sunday

'Perry stirs your conscience as well as your soul'

Northern Echo

'The novel has a totally contemporary feel and is admirably well-written'

Guardian

'Perry's characters are richly drawn and the plot satisfyingly serpentine'

Booklist

'A beauty: brilliantly presented, ingeniously developed and packed with political implications that reverberate on every level of British society . . . delivers Perry's most harrowing insights into the secret lives of the elegant Victorians who hav

k Review

By Anne Perry and available from Headline

The Christmas Novella series
A Christmas Journey
A Christmas Visitor
A Christmas Guest
A Christmas Secret
A Christmas Beginning
A Christmas Grace

World War I series
No Graves as Yet
Shoulder the Sky
Angels in the Gloom
At Some Disputed Barricade
We Shall Not Sleep

The Inspector Pitt series
Bedford Square
Half Moon Street
The Whitechapel Conspiracy
Southampton Row
Seven Dials
Long Spoon Lane
Buckingham Palace Gardens

The William Monk series
The Face of a Stranger
A Dangerous Mourning
Defend and Betray
A Sudden, Fearful Death
The Sins of the Wolf
Cain His Brother
Weighed in the Balance
The Silent Cry
Whited Sepulchres
The Twisted Root
Slaves and Obsession
A Funeral in Blue
Death of a Stranger
The Shifting Tide
Dark Assassin
Execution Dock

Tathea
Come Armaggedon
The One Thing More

A CHRISTMAS GRACE

Anne Perry

headline

First published in Great Britain in 2008 by
HEADLINE PUBLISHING GROUP

First published in paperback in Great Britain in 2009 by
HEADLINE PUBLISHING GROUP

1

Cataloguing in Publication Data is available from the British Library

ISBN 978 0 7553 3433 9

Typeset in Times by Palimpsest Book Production Limited,
Grangemouth, Stirlingshire

Printed and bound in Great Britain by
Printed in the UK by CPI Mackays, Chatham ME5 8TD

Headline's policy is to use papers that are natural, renewable and recyclable products and made from wood grown in sustainable forests. The logging and manufacturing processes are expected to conform to the environmental regulations of the country of origin.

HEADLINE PUBLISHING GROUP
An Hachette UK Company
338 Euston Road
London NW1 3BH

www.headline.co.uk
www.hachette.co.uk

Dedicated to all who long for a Second Chance

Emily Radley stood in the centre of her magnificent withdrawing room and considered where she should have the Christmas tree placed so that it would show to the best advantage. The decorations were already planned: the bows, the coloured balls, the tinsel, the little glass icicles and the red and green shiny birds. At the foot would be the brightly wrapped presents for her husband and children.

All through the house there would be candles, wreaths and garlands of holly and ivy. There would be bowls of crystallised fruit and porcelain dishes of nuts, jugs of mulled wine, plates of mince pies, roasted chestnuts, and, of course, great fires in the hearths with apple logs to burn with a sweet smell.

The year of 1895 had not been an easy one, and she was happy enough to see it come to a close. Because they were staying in London, rather than going to the country, there would be parties, and dinners, including the Duchess of Warwick's; everyone she knew would be at that. And there would be balls where they would dance all night. She had her gown chosen: the palest possible green, embroidered with gold. And, of course, there was the theatre. It would not be the same without anything of Oscar Wilde's, but there would be Goldsmith's *She Stoops to Conquer*, and that was fun.

She was still thinking about it when Jack came in. He looked a little tired, but he had the same easy grace of manner as always. He was holding a letter in his hand.

'Post?' she asked in surprise. 'At this time in the evening?' Her heart sank. 'It's not some government matter, is it? They can't want you now. It's less than three weeks till Christmas.'

'It's for you,' he replied, holding it out for her. 'It was just delivered. I think it's Thomas's handwriting.'

Thomas Pitt was Emily's brother-in-law, a policeman. Her sister Charlotte had married considerably beneath her. She had not regretted it for a day, even if it had cost her the social and financial comforts she had been accustomed to. On the contrary, it was Emily who envied Charlotte the opportunities she had been given to involve herself in some of his cases. It seemed like far too long since Emily had shared an adventure, the danger, the emotion, the anger and the pity. Somehow she felt less alive for it.

She tore open the envelope and read the paper inside.

Dear Emily,

I am very sorry to tell you that Charlotte received a letter today from a Roman Catholic priest, Father

Tyndale, who lives in a small village in the Connemara region of Western Ireland. He is the pastor to Susannah Ross, your father's younger sister. She is now widowed again, and Father Tyndale says she is very ill. In fact this will certainly be her last Christmas.

I know she parted from the family in less than happy circumstances, but we should not allow her to be alone at such a time. Your mother is in Italy, and unfortunately Charlotte has a bad case of bronchitis, which is why I am writing to ask you if you will go to Ireland to be with Susannah. I realise it is a great sacrifice, but there is no one else.

Father Tyndale says it cannot be for long, and you would be most welcome in Susannah's home. If you write back to him at the enclosed address, he will meet you at the Galway station from whichever train you say. Please make it within a day or two. There is little time to hesitate.

I thank you in advance, and Charlotte sends her love. She will write to you when she is well enough.

Yours with gratitude,

Thomas

Emily looked up and met Jack's eyes. 'It's preposterous!' she exclaimed. 'He's lost his wits.'

Jack blinked. 'Really. What does he say?'

Wordlessly she passed the letter to him.

He read it, frowning, and then offered it back to her. 'I'm

sorry. I know you were looking forward to Christmas at home, but there'll be another one next year.'

'I'm not going!' she said incredulously.

He said nothing, just looked at her steadily.

'It's ridiculous,' she protested. 'I can't go to Connemara, for heaven's sake. Especially not at Christmas. It'll be like the end of the world. In fact it is the end of the world. Jack, it's nothing but freezing bog.'

'Actually I believe the west coast of Ireland is quite temperate,' he corrected her. 'But wet, of course,' he added with a smile.

She breathed out a sigh of relief. His smile could still charm her more than she wished him to know. If he did, he might be impossible to manage at all. She turned away to put the letter on the table. 'I'll write to Thomas tomorrow and explain to him.'

'What will you say?' he asked.

She was surprised. 'That it's out of the question, of course. But I'll put it nicely.'

'How nicely can you say that you'll let your aunt die alone at Christmas because you don't fancy the Irish climate?' he asked, his voice surprisingly gentle, considering the words.

Emily froze. She turned back to look at him, and knew that in spite of the smile, he meant exactly what he had said. 'Do you really want me to go away to Ireland for the entire Christmas?' she asked. 'Susannah's only fifty. She might live for ages. He doesn't even say what's wrong with her.'

'One can die at any age,' Jack pointed out. 'And what I would like has nothing to do with what is right.'

'What about the children?' Emily played the trump card. 'What will they think if I leave them for Christmas? It is a time when families should be together.' She smiled back at him.

'Then write and tell your aunt to die alone because you want to be with your family,' he replied. 'On second thoughts, you'll have to tell the priest, and he can tell her.'

The appalling realisation hit her. 'You want me to go!' she accused him.

'No, I don't,' he denied. 'But neither do I want to live with you all the years afterwards when Susannah is dead, and you wish you had done. Guilt can destroy even the dearest things. In fact, especially the dearest.' He reached out and touched her cheek gently. 'I don't want to lose you.'

'You won't!' she said quickly. 'You'll never lose me.'

'Lots of people lose each other.' He shook his head. 'Some people even lose themselves.'

She looked down at the carpet. 'But it's Christmas!'

He did not answer.

The seconds ticked by. The fire crackled in the hearth.

'Do you suppose they have telegrams in Ireland?' she asked finally.

'I've no idea. What can you possibly say in a telegram that would answer this?'

She took a deep breath. 'What time my train gets into Galway. And on what day, I suppose.'

He leaned forward and kissed her very gently, and she found she was crying, for all that she would miss over the next weeks, and all that she thought Christmas ought to be.

But two days later, when the train finally pulled into Galway a little before noon and Emily stepped out onto the platform in the fine rain, she was in an entirely different frame of mind. She was stiff, and extremely tired after a rough crossing of the Irish Sea and a night in a Dublin hotel. If Jack had had the remotest idea what he was asking of her, he wouldn't have been nearly so cavalier about it. This was a sacrifice no one should ask. It was Susannah's choice to have turned her back on her family, married a Roman Catholic no one knew, and decided to live out here in the bog and the rain. She had not come home when Emily's father was dying! Of course, no one had asked her to. In fact, Emily admitted to herself reluctantly, it was quite possible no one had even told her he was ill.

The porter unloaded her luggage and put it on the platform. She had not asked him to – it was quite unnecessary. This was the end of the line, in every possible sense.

She paid him to take it out to the street, and followed him along the platform, getting wetter every minute. She was in the roadway when she saw a pony and trap, a priest standing very conspicuously talking to the animal. He turned as he heard the porter's trolley on the cobbles. He saw Emily and his face lit with a broad smile. He was a plain man, his features unremarkable, a little lumpy, and yet in that moment he was beautiful.

'Ah,' he came forward with his hand out, 'Mrs Radley. Surely it is very good of you to come all this way, and at this time of the year. Was your crossing very bad? God put a rough sea between you and me, to make us all the more grateful to arrive safely on the further shore. A bit like life.' He shrugged ruefully, his eyes for a moment filled with sadness. 'How are you, then? Tired and cold? And it's a long journey we have yet, but there's no help for it.' He looked her up and down with sympathy. 'Unless you're not well enough to make it today?'

'Thank you, Father Tyndale, but I'm quite well enough,' Emily replied. She was about to ask how long it could be, then changed her mind. He might take it for faint-heartedness.

'Ah, I'm delighted,' he said quickly. 'Now let's get your cases up here into the back, and we'll set off then. We'll make most of the way in daylight, so we will.' He turned and picked up one of the cases, and with a mighty heave set it on the back of the cart. The porter was barely quick enough to get the lighter one up by himself.

Emily drew in her breath to say something, then changed her mind. What was there to say? It was midday, and he did not think he would reach Susannah's house before nightfall! What benighted end of the world were they going to?

Father Tyndale helped her up into the cart on the seat beside him, tucked a rug around her, and a waterproof cloth after that, then went briskly round and climbed in the other side. After a word of encouragement the pony set off at a steady walk. Emily had a hideous feeling that the animal knew a lot more about it than she did, and was pacing itself for a long journey.

As they left the town the rain eased a little and Emily started to look around at the rolling land. There were sudden vistas of hills in the distance to the west as the clouds parted and occasional shreds of blue sky appeared. Shafts of light gleamed on wet grasslands, which seemed to have layers of colour, wind bleached on top but with a depth of sullen reds and scorched greens below. There was a lot of shadow on the lee side of the hills, peat-dark streams, and the occasional ruin of an old stone shelter, now almost black except where the sun glistened on the wet surfaces.

'In a few minutes you'll see the lake,' Father Tyndale said suddenly. 'Very beautiful it is, and lots of fish in it, and birds. You'll like it. Quite different from the sea, of course.'

'Yes, of course,' Emily agreed, huddling closer into her blanket. She felt as if she should say more. He was looking resolutely ahead, concentrating on his driving, although she wondered why. There was nowhere else to go but the winding road ahead, and the pony seemed to know its way perfectly well. If Father Tyndale had tied the reins to the iron hold provided, and fallen asleep, he would no doubt have got home just as safely. Still, the silence required something.

'You said that my aunt is very ill,' she began tentatively. 'I have no experience in nursing. What will I be able to do for her?'

'Don't let it worry you, Mrs Radley,' Father Tyndale replied with a softness in his voice. 'For sure Mrs O'Bannion will be there to help. Death will come when it will. There's nothing to do to change that, simply a little care in the meantime.'

'Is . . . is she in a lot of pain?'

'No, not so much, at least of body. And the doctor comes when he can. It's more a heaviness of the spirit, a remembrance of things past . . .' He gave a long sigh and there was a slight shadow in his face, not a change in the light so much as something from within. 'There are regrets, things that need doing before it's too late,' he added. 'That's so for all of us, it's just that the knowledge that you have little time makes it more pressing, you understand?'

'Yes,' Emily said bleakly, thinking back to the ugly parting when Susannah had informed the family that she was going to marry again, not to anyone they approved of, but to an Irishman who lived in Connemara. That in itself was not serious. The offence was that Hugo Ross was Roman Catholic.

Emily had asked at the time why on earth that mattered so much, but her father had been too angry and too hurt over what he saw as his sister's defection to pursue the subject of history and the disloyalties of the past.

Now Emily stared at the bleak landscape. The wind rippled through the long grasses, bending them so the shadows made them look like water. Wild birds flew overhead; she counted at least a dozen different kinds. There were hardly any trees, just wet land glistening in the occasional shafts of sun, a view now and then of the lake that Father Tyndale had spoken of, long reeds growing at the edges like black knifemarks. There was little sound but the pony's hoofs on the road, and the sighing of the wind.

What did Susannah regret? Her marriage? Losing touch with her own family? Coming here as a stranger to this place at the end of the world? It was too late to change now, whatever it was. Susannah's husband and Emily's father were both dead; there was nothing to say to anyone that would matter. Did she want someone from the past here simply so she could feel that one of them cared? Or would she say that she loved them, and she was sorry?

They must have been travelling for at least an hour. It felt like more. Emily was cold and stiff, and a good deal of her was also wet.

They passed the first crossroads she had seen, and she was disappointed when they did not take either turning. She asked Father Tyndale about it.

'Moycullen,' he replied with the ghost of a smile. 'The left goes to Spiddal, and the sea, but it's the long way round. This is much faster. In about another hour we'll be at Oughterard, and we'll stop there for a bite to eat. You'll be ready, no doubt.'

Another hour! However long was this journey? She

swallowed. 'Yes, thank you. That would be very nice. Then where?'

'Oh, it's a little westwards to Maam Cross, then south around the coast through Roundstone, and a few more miles and we're there,' he replied.

Emily could think of nothing to say.

Oughterard proved to be warmly welcoming and the food was delicious, eaten in a dining room with an enormous peat fire. It gave off not only more heat than she would have imagined, but an earthy, smoky aroma she found extremely pleasing. She was offered a glass of something mildly alcoholic, which looked like river water but tasted acceptable enough, and she left feeling as if so long as she did not count the time or the miles, she might survive the rest of the way.

They passed Maam Cross and the weather cleared as the afternoon faded. There was a distinct gold in the air when Father Tyndale pointed out the Maumturk Mountains in the north east.

'We never met Susannah's husband,' Emily said suddenly. 'What was he like?'

Father Tyndale smiled. 'Oh, now that was a shame,' he replied with feeling. 'A fine man, he was. Quiet, you know, for an Irishman. But when he told a story you listened, and when he laughed you laughed with him. Loved the land, and painted it like no one else. Gave it a light so you could smell the air of it just by looking. But you'll maybe be knowing that yourself?'

'No,' Emily said with amazement. 'I . . . I didn't even know he was an artist.' She felt ashamed. 'We thought he had some kind of family money. Not a lot, but enough to live on.'

Father Tyndale laughed. It was a rich, happy sound in the empty land where she could hear only bird cries, wind, and the pony's feet on the road. 'That's true enough, but we judge a man by his soul, not his pocket,' he answered her. 'Hugo painted for the love of it.'

'What did he look like?' she asked. Then she felt self-conscious for thinking of something so trivial, and wanted Father Tyndale to understand the reason. 'Just so I can picture him. When you think of someone, you get an idea in your head. I want it to be right.'

'He was a big man,' Father Tyndale replied thoughtfully. 'He had brown hair that curled, and blue eyes. He was happy, that's what I remember he looked like. And he had beautiful hands, as if he could touch anything without hurting it.'

With no warning at all, Emily found herself almost on the edge of tears that she would never meet Hugo Ross. She must be very tired. She had been travelling for two days, and she had no idea what sort of a place she was going to, or how Susannah would be changed by time and illness, not to mention years of estrangement from the family. This whole journey was ridiculous. She shouldn't have allowed Jack to talk her into coming.

It was over four hours now since they had left Galway. 'How much longer will it be?' she asked the priest.

'Not more than another two hours,' he replied cheerfully. 'That's the Twelve Fins over there,' he pointed to a row of hills now almost straight to the north. 'And the Lake of Ballynahinch ahead. We'll turn off before then, down towards the shore, then past Roundstone, and we're there.'

They stopped at another hotel, and ate more excellent food. Afterwards it was even more difficult going out into the dusk and a damp wind from the west.

Then the sky cleared and as they crested a slight rise the view opened up in front of them, the sun spilled across the water in a blaze of scarlet and gold, black headlands seeming to jut up out of liquid fire. From the look of it, the road before them could have been inlaid with bronze. Emily could smell the salt in the air and, looking up a moment, her eye caught the pale underside of birds circling, riding the wind in the last light.

Father Tyndale smiled and said nothing, but she knew he had heard her sharp intake of breath.

'Tell me something about the village,' she said when the sun had almost disappeared and she knew the pony must be finding its way largely by habit, knowing it was almost home.

It was several moments before he answered, and when he did she heard a note of sadness in his voice, as if he were being called to account for some mistake he had made.

'It's smaller than it was,' he said. 'Too many of our young people go away now.' He stopped, seeming lost for further words.

Emily felt embarrassed. This was a land in which neither she nor her countrymen had any business, yet they had been here for centuries. She was made welcome because they were hospitable by nature. But what did they really feel? What had it been like for Susannah coming here? Little wonder she was desperate enough to ask a Catholic priest to beg anyone of her family to be with her for her last days.

She cleared her throat. 'Actually I was rather thinking of the houses, the streets, the people you know . . . that sort of thing.'

'You'll meet them, for sure,' he answered. 'Mrs Ross is well liked. They'll call, even if only briefly, not to tire her, poor soul. She used to walk miles along the shore, or over towards the Roundstone Bog, especially in the spring. She went with Hugo when he took his paints. Just sat and read a book, or went looking for the wildflowers. But the sea was the best for her. Never grew tired of looking at it. She was collecting some papers about the Martin family, but I don't know if she kept up with that after she fell ill.'

'Who are the Martins?' Emily asked.

His face cleared. 'Oh, the Martins are part of the Rosses, or the other way around,' he said with pride. 'Once it was the Flahertys and the Conneeleys that ruled the area. Fought each other to a standstill, so they did. But there are still Flahertys in the village, for all that, and Conneeleys too, of course. And others you'll meet. But for history, Padraic Yorke is the one. He knows everything there is to know, and tells it with the music of the land in his voice, and the laughter and tears of the people.'

'I must meet him, if I can.'

'He'll be happy to tell you where everything happened, and the names of the flowers and the birds. Not that they're so many at this time of year.'

She imagined she would have no time for such things, but she thanked him anyway.

They arrived a little after six in the evening, and it was already pitch-dark, with a haze of rain obscuring the stars to the east. But clear in the west there was a low moon, sufficient to see the outline of the village. They drove through, and on to Susannah's house beyond – closer to the shore.

Father Tyndale alighted and knocked on the front door. It was several minutes before it opened and Susannah was silhouetted against a blaze of candlelight. She must have had at least a dozen lit. She came out onto the step, peering beyond Father Tyndale as if to make sure there was someone else with him.

Emily walked over the gravel and up the wide entrance paving into the light.

'Emily . . .' Susannah said softly. 'You look wonderful, but you must be very tired. Thank you so much for coming.'

Emily stepped forward. 'Aunt Susannah.' It seemed absurd to say very much more. She was tired, as must be clear, but looking at Susannah's gaunt face and her body so obviously fragile, even under a woollen dress and shawl, it would be childish even to think of herself. And to ask how Susannah was would seem to trivialise what they both knew to be the truth.

'It was an excellent journey,' she lied. 'And Father Tyndale has been most kind to me.'

'You must be cold and hungry.' Susannah stepped back into the light. 'And wet,' she added.

Emily was shocked. She remembered Susannah as interesting more than pretty, but with good features and a truly beautiful skin, like her own. The woman she saw now was haggard, the bones of her face prominent, her eyes sunken in shadowed sockets.

'A little,' Emily said, trying to force her voice to sound normal. 'But it will soon mend. A night's sleep will make all the difference.' She felt an urgent temptation to talk too much in order to fill the yawning silence.

Susannah looked at Father Tyndale and Emily suddenly became aware that she must be finding it hard to stand here at the door in the cold.

Father Tyndale set the cases down just inside. 'Would you like me to take them upstairs?' he asked.

Emily knew it would be next to impossible for her to carry the larger one, so she accepted.

Five minutes later Father Tyndale was gone and Emily and Susannah stood alone in the hall. Now it was awkward. There was a barrier of ten years' silence between them. It was duty that brought Emily, and she could not pretend affection. Had she cared, they would have corresponded during that time. Susannah must feel the same.

'Supper is ready,' Susannah said with a faint smile. 'I imagine you would like to retire early.'

'Thank you. Yes.' Emily followed her across the chilly hallway into a wood-panelled dining room whose warmth embraced her the moment she was through the door. A peat fire in the huge stone hearth did not dance with flame, like the fires she was used to at home, but its sweet, earthy aroma filled the air. There were candles burning in all the holders, and a polished wooden table was set for two. There was no sign of any servant. Perhaps there was none resident. Emily had a sudden, sinking fear that in spite of what Father Tyndale had said, she might have more duties than she had expected, and for which she was ill equipped.

'May I help?' she said tentatively. Decency required it.

Susannah gave her a glance with unexpected humour. 'I didn't ask you here to be a servant, Emily. Mrs O'Bannion does all the heavy work, and I can still cook, adequately at least. I pick the times of day when I feel best.' She stood in the doorway leading to the kitchen. 'I wanted someone here who was of my own family, you or Charlotte.' The light vanished from her face. 'There are things to see to before I die.' She turned and went out, leaving the door open behind her, perhaps so she could return with both hands full.

Emily was relieved that Susannah had gone before any reply to that last remark was necessary. When she came back with a tureen of stew, and then a dish of mashed potatoes, it was easy to let the previous conversation slip.

The stew was excellent, and Emily was happy enough to enjoy it, and then the apple pie that followed. They spoke of trivialities. Emily realised that she hardly knew Susannah. Being aware of the facts of someone's life is quite different from understanding even their opinions, let alone their dreams. Susannah was her father's sister, and yet they were strangers sitting across a table, alone with each other, at the edge of the world. Outside the wind sighed in the eaves and rain splattered the glass.

'Tell me about the village,' Emily asked, unable to let the silence extend. 'It was too dark to see much on my way through.'

Susannah smiled, but there was a sharp sadness in her eyes. 'I don't know that there's anything different about them, except that they're my people. Their griefs matter to me.' She looked down at the table with its gleaming surface, close grained and polished like silk. 'Perhaps you'll come to know them, and then I won't need to explain. Hugo loved them, in the quiet way you do when something is part of your life.' She took a deep breath and looked up, forcing herself to smile. 'Would you like anything more to eat?'

'No thank you,' Emily said quickly. 'I have eaten excellently. Either you or Mrs O'Bannion is an excellent cook.'

'I am with pastry, not much else,' Susannah replied. She smiled, but she looked desperately tired. 'Thank you for coming, Emily. I'm sure you would rather have spent Christmas at home. Please don't feel it necessary to deny that. I am perfectly aware of how much I am asking of you. Still, I hope you will be comfortable here, and warm enough. There is a fire in your bedroom, and peat in the box to replenish it. It's better not to let it go out. They can be hard to start again.' She rose to her feet slowly, as if trying to make sure she did not sway or stumble. 'Now, if you will excuse me, I think I will go upstairs. Please leave everything as it is. Mrs O'Bannion will see to it when she comes in the morning.'

Emily slept so well she barely moved in the bed, but when she woke to hear the wind gusting around the eaves she was momentarily confused as to where she was. She sat up and saw the embers of the fire before she remembered with a jolt that there was no maid to help. She had better restoke it quickly, before it died completely.

Surprisingly, when she was out of bed the air was not as chill as she had expected. When the new peat was on the fire, she opened the curtains and stared at the sight that met her eyes. The panorama was breathtaking. The sky was a turmoil of clouds, rolling in like a wild reflection of the sea below, white spume topping the waves, grey water heaving. Far to the right was a long headland of dark, jagged rocks. Below was a sandy shore with the tide high and threatening. To the left the land was softer, stretching away in alternate sand and rock until it disappeared in a belt of rain and the outlines melted into one another. It was fierce, elemental, but there was a beauty about it that no static landscape could match.

She washed in the water that had been left in a ewer beside the fire, and was quite pleasantly warm, and dressed in a morning gown of plain, dark green. Then she went downstairs to see if Susannah were awake, and if she might like any assistance.

In the kitchen she found a handsome woman in her late thirties with shining brown hair and dark-lashed eyes of a curious blue-green colour. She smiled as soon as she realised Emily was there.

'Good morning to you,' she said cheerfully. 'You'll be Mrs Radley. Welcome to Connemara.'

'Thank you.' Emily walked into the warm, spacious kitchen, her feet suddenly noisy on the stone floor. 'Mrs O'Bannion?'

The woman smiled broadly. 'I am. And that's Bridie you can hear barging about in the scullery. Never known such a girl for making a noise. What'd you like for breakfast, now? How about scrambled eggs on toast, an' a nice pot of tea?'

'Perfect, thank you. How is Mrs Ross?'

Maggie O'Bannion's face shadowed. 'She'll not be down yet for a while, the poor soul. Sometimes mornings are good for her, but more often they're not.'

'Is there anything I can do to help?' Emily asked, feeling foolish and yet compelled to offer.

'Enjoy your breakfast,' Maggie replied. 'If you want to

take a breath of air, I'd do it soon. The wind's rising fit to tear the sky to pieces, and it's best you're well inside the house when it gets bad.'

Emily looked at the window. 'Thank you. I'll take your advice, but it doesn't look unpleasant.'

Maggie shivered, her lips pressed together. 'There's a keening in the wind. I can hear it.' She turned away and began to prepare breakfast for Emily.

Susannah came down at about ten. She was pale faced, and there was more grey in her hair than Emily had appreciated in the warmth of the previous evening's candlelight. However, she seemed rested and her smile was quick when she saw Emily in the drawing room writing letters.

'Did you sleep well? I hope you were comfortable? Did Maggie get you breakfast?'

Emily stood up. 'Excellent to all of the questions,' she replied. 'And Mrs O'Bannion is charming, and I have eaten very well, thank you. You are quite right, I like her already.'

Susannah glanced at the notepaper. 'May I suggest you take them to the post before lunch? I think the wind is rising.' She gave a quick look towards the window. 'We might be in for a bad storm. They can happen this time of the year. Sometimes they are very dreadful.'

Emily did not reply. It seemed an odd remark to make. Everybody had storms in the winter. It was part of life. As far as she had heard, they did not have the snow in Connemara that they did in England.

She returned to her letters and at eleven o'clock she joined Susannah and Maggie for a mug of cocoa. With the wind whining outside and occasional gusts of rain on the glass, sitting at the kitchen table with biscuits and a hot cup in her hands seemed almost like revisiting the comforts of childhood.

A twig clattered against the window and Maggie turned quickly to stare at it. Susannah's thin hands clenched on the porcelain of her cup. She drew in her breath sharply.

Maggie looked away, meeting Emily's eyes and forcing herself to smile. 'We'll be quite warm inside,' she said unnecessarily. 'And there's enough peat cut to last into January.'

Emily wanted to make some light remark to relieve the tension with laughter, but she could not think of anything. She realised that she did not know either of these women well enough to understand why they were afraid. What did a little wind matter?

But in the middle of the afternoon the sky darkened with heavy clouds to the west and the wind was considerably fiercer. Emily did not realise just how hard it was until she went outside to clip a handful of red willow twigs to add to the bowl of holly and ivy in the hall. It was not as cold as she had expected, but the force of the gale whipped her skirt as if it had been a sail, carrying her backwards off balance. It was a moment before she steadied herself and leaned into it.

'Be careful, ma'am,' a man's voice said, so close she spun round, startled, as if he had threatened her.

He was almost ten feet away, a large man with blunt features and dark, troubled eyes. He smiled at her tentatively, no lightness in his expression.

'I'm sorry,' Emily apologised for her overreaction. 'I hadn't expected the wind to be so hard.'

'Sure, it's going to get worse,' the man said gently, raising his voice only just enough to be heard. He looked up at the sky, narrowing his eyes.

'Are you looking for Mrs Ross?' Emily asked him.

He spread his hands in a gesture of apology. 'An' I have no manners at all. I'm thinking because I know you're Mrs Ross's niece, that you must know me too. I'm Fergal O'Bannion. I've come to walk Maggie home.' Again he looked at the sky, but this time westwards, towards the sea.

'Do you live far away?' She was disappointed. She liked Maggie and had hoped she lived close by and would be able to come to Susannah even in the worst of the winter. Otherwise Susannah would be very much alone, especially as her illness became worse.

'Over there,' Fergal pointed to what appeared to be little more than half a mile away.

'Oh.' Emily could think of no answer that made sense, so she merely smiled. 'I'm just going to cut a few twigs. Please go in. I'm sure Mrs O'Bannion is just about ready.'

He thanked her and went inside, and Emily went to look for bright, unblemished stems. She was puzzled. What could Fergal possibly be afraid of that he came to walk Maggie home for less than a mile? There was no imaginable danger. It must be something else – a village feud, perhaps?

She found the twigs and returned to the house five minutes later. Maggie was in the hallway putting her shawl on and Fergal was waiting by the door.

'Thank you,' Susannah said with a quick smile at Maggie.

Emily laid the twigs on the hall table.

'I'll be back in the morning,' Maggie told them. 'I'll bring bread, and a few eggs.'

'If the weather holds,' Fergal qualified.

She shot him a sharp glance, and then bit her lip and turned to face Susannah. 'Of course it'll hold, at least enough for that. I won't let you down,' she promised Susannah.

'Maggie—' Fergal began.

'Course I won't,' Maggie repeated, then smiled warningly at her husband. 'Come on. Let's be going, then. What are you waiting for?' She opened the front door and strode out into the wind. It caught her skirts, billowing them out and making her lose her balance very slightly. Fergal went after her, catching up in a couple of strides and putting his arm around her to steady her a moment before Maggie leaned into him.

Emily closed the front door. 'Shall I get us a cup of tea?' she offered. She had missed her chance to take her letters to the post today. They would have to go tomorrow.

Fifteen minutes later they were sitting by the fire, tea tray on the low table between them.

Emily swallowed a mouthful of shortbread. 'Why is Fergal so worried about the weather? It's a bit blustery, but that's all. I'll walk with Maggie, if it'll make her feel better.'

'It isn't—' Susannah began, then stopped, looking down at her plate. 'Storms can be bad here.'

'Enough to blow a sturdy woman off her feet in half a mile of roadway?' Emily said incredulously.

Susannah drew in her breath, then let it out without answering. Emily considered what it was she had been going to say, and why she had changed her mind. But Susannah evaded the subject all evening, and went to bed early.

'Good night,' she said to Emily, standing in the doorway with a faint smile. Her face was lined and bleak, the hollows around her eyes almost blue in the shadows, as if she were at the end of a very long road and had little strength left. There was no real reason why, but Emily had the impression that she was afraid.

'If you need me for anything, please call,' Emily offered quietly. 'Even if it's just to fetch something for you. I'm not a guest, I'm family.'

There were sudden tears in Susannah's eyes. 'Thank you,' she replied, turning away.

Emily slept well again, tired by the newness of her surroundings and the distress of realising how very ill Susannah was. Father Tyndale had said that she was not going to live much longer, but that conveyed little of the real pain of dying. At only fifty she was far too young to waste away like this. She must have so much more yet to do, and to enjoy.

Emily got up too early to make breakfast for Susannah. She had no idea how long to wait. She made herself a cup of tea in the kitchen, listening to the wind buffeting the house, occasionally rising to a shrill whine around the edges of the roof.

She decided to explore. There did not seem to be any part of the house that was specifically private; no doors were locked. She wandered from the dining room to the library, where there were several hundred books. She looked at titles and picked randomly off the shelves. It did not take her long to realise that at least half of them had been Hugo Ross's. His name was written on the flyleaves. They were on subjects Emily suspected Susannah might never have read without his influence: archaeology, exploration, animals of the sea, tides and currents, several histories of Ireland. There were also volumes on philosophy, and many of the great novels not only of England but also of Russia and France.

She began to regret that she would never meet the man who had collected these, and so clearly enjoyed them.

She looked on the mantelshelf, and the small semicircular table against the wall. There were cut-crystal candlesticks that might have been Susannah's, and a meerschaum pipe that could only have been Hugo's. It was left as if he had just put it down, not gone years ago.

There were other things, including a silver-framed photograph of a family group outside a low cottage, the Connemara hills behind them.

Emily went next into Hugo's study. There were haunting seascapes on the walls and there was still pipe tobacco in the humidor, an incomplete list of colours on a slip of paper, as if a reminder for buying paints. Had Susannah deliberately left these things because she wanted to pretend that he would come back? Perhaps she had loved him enough that it was not death she was afraid of, but something quite different, something against which there was also no protection.

If Jack had died, would Emily have done the same – left memories of him in the house, as if his life were so woven into hers that it could not be torn out? She did not want to answer that. If it were, how could she bear losing him? If it were not, then what fullness of love had she missed?

She went back to the kitchen, made breakfast of boiled eggs and fingers of toast, and took Susannah's upstairs for her. It was a fine day and the wind seemed to be easing. She decided to take her letters to the post office now. 'I won't be more than an hour,' she promised. 'Can I bring you anything?'

Susannah thanked her but declined, and Emily set out along the road by the shore, which led a mile and a half or so to the village shop. The sky was almost clear and there was a strange, invigorating smell that she had not experienced before, a mixture of salt and aromatic plants of some kind. It was both bitter and pleasing. To her left the land seemed desolate all the way to the hills on the skyline, and yet there were always wind patterns in the grass and layers of colour beneath the surface.

To her right the sea had a deep swell, the smooth backs of the waves heavy and hard, sending white-spumed tongues up the sand. There were headlands to either side, but directly out from the shore for as far as she could see there was only the restless water.

Gulls wheeled in the air above her, their cries blending with the sighing of the wind in the grass and the constant sound of the waves. She walked a little faster, and found herself smiling for no apparent reason. If this was what the local people thought of as a storm, it was nothing!

She reached the low, straggling houses of the village, mostly stone built and looking as if they had grown out of the land itself. She crossed the wiry turf to the roadway and continued along it until she came to the small shop. Inside there were two other people waiting to be served and a small, plump woman behind the counter weighing out sugar and putting it into a blue bag. Behind her the shelves were stacked with all kinds of goods – groceries, hardware, and occasional household linens.

They all stopped talking and turned to look at Emily.

'Good morning,' she said cheerfully. 'I'm Emily Radley, niece of Mrs Ross. I've come to spend Christmas with her.'

'Ah, niece, is it?' a tall, gaunt woman said with a smile, pushing grey-blonde hair back into its pins with one hand. 'My neighbour's granddaughter said you'd come.'

Emily was lost.

'Bridie Molloy,' the woman explained. 'I'm Kathleen.'

'How do you do?' Emily replied, uncertain how to address her.

'I'm Mary O'Donnell,' the woman behind the counter said. 'What can I be doing to help you?'

Emily hesitated. She knew it was unacceptable to push ahead of others. Then she realised they were curious to see what she would ask for. She smiled. 'I have only letters to post,' she said. 'Just to let my family know that I arrived safely, and have met with great kindness. Even the weather is very mild. I fancy it will be much colder at home.'

The women looked at each other, then back at Emily.

'Nice enough now, but it's coming,' Kathleen said grimly.

Mary O'Donnell agreed with her, and the third woman, younger, with tawny-red hair, bit her lip and nodded her head. 'It'll be a hard one,' she said with a shiver. 'I can hear it in the wind.'

'Same time o' the year,' Kathleen said quietly. 'Exact.'

'The wind has died down,' Emily told them.

Again they looked at each other.

'It's the quiet before it hits,' Mary O'Donnell said softly. 'You'll see. The real one's out there waiting.' She pointed towards the west and the trackless enormity of the ocean. 'I'll have your letters, then. We'd best get them on their way, while we can.'

Emily was a trifle taken aback, but she thanked her, paid

the postage, and wished them good day. Outside again in the bright air, she started along the path back, and almost immediately saw ahead of her the slender figure of a man with his head turned towards the sea, walking slowly and every now and then stopping. Without hurrying she caught up with him.

At a distance, because of the ease with which he moved, she had thought him young, but now that she could see his face she realised he was probably sixty. His hair flying in the wind was faded and his keen face deeply lined. When he looked at her his eyes were a bright grey.

'You must be Susannah's niece. Don't be surprised,' he observed with amusement. 'It's a small village. An incomer is news. And we are all fond of Susannah. She wouldn't have been without friends for Christmas, but that isn't the same as family.'

Emily felt defensive, as if she and Charlotte had been to blame for Susannah's situation. 'She was the one who moved away,' she replied, then instantly thought how childish that sounded. 'Unfortunately after my father died, we didn't keep in touch as we should have.'

He smiled back at her. 'It happens. Women follow the men they love, and distances can be hard to cross.'

They were standing on the shore, the wind tugging at their hair and clothes, rough but mild, no cruelty in it. She thought the waves were a little steeper than when she had set out, but perhaps she was merely closer to them here on the sand.

'I'm glad she was happy here,' she said impulsively. 'Did you know her husband?'

'Of course,' he replied. 'We all know each other here, and have done for generations – the Martins, the Rosses, the Conneeleys, the Flahertys. The Rosses and Martins are all one, of course. The Conneeleys and the Flahertys also, but in an entirely different way. But perhaps you know that?'

'No, not at all?' she lifted her voice to make it a question.

He did not need a second invitation. 'Years ago, last century, the Flahertys murdered all of the Conneeleys, except Una Conneeley. She escaped alive, with the child she was carrying. When he was born and grew up he starved himself to force her to tell him the truth of his birth.' He glanced at her to make sure she was listening.

'Go on,' Emily prompted. She was in no hurry to be back inside the house again. She watched the seabirds careening up the corridors of the wind. The smell of salt was strong in the air and the surf pounding now white on the shore, gave her a sense of exhilaration, almost of freedom.

'Well, she told him, of course,' he continued, his eyes bright. 'And when he was fully grown he came back here and found the Flaherty tyrant of the day living on an island in a lake near Bunowen.' His face was vivid as if he recalled it himself. 'Conneeley measured the distance from the shore to the island, and then set two stones apart on the hillside, that exact space, and practised until he could make the jump.'

'Yes?' she urged.

He was delighted to go on. 'Flaherty's daughter nearly drowned in the lake and young Conneeley rescued her. They fell in love. He jumped the water to the island and stabbed Flaherty's eyes out.'

Emily winced.

He grinned. 'And when the blind man then offered to shake his hand, the girl gave her lover a horse's leg bone to offer instead of his hand, which shows she knew her father very well. Flaherty crushed it to powder with his grip. Conneeley killed him on the spot, and he and Flaherty's daughter lived happily ever after – starting the whole new clan, which now peoples the neighbourhood.'

'Really?' She had no idea if he was even remotely serious; then she saw the fire of emotion in his face and knew that, for all his lightness of telling, he was speaking of passions that were woven into the very meaning of his life. 'I see,' she added, so that he would know she understood its validity.

'Padraic Yorke,' he said, holding out his thin, strong hand.

'Emily Radley,' she replied, taking it warmly.

'Oh, I know,' he nodded. 'Indirectly you are part of our history here, because you are Susannah's niece, and Susannah was Hugo Ross's wife.' His voice dropped. 'It hasn't been the same since he died.'

She should have felt this was slightly imprisoning, but actually she was happy to be part of this enormous, wind-torn land, just for a season, and of its people who knew each other with such fierce intimacy.

Padraic Yorke started walking again, and she kept pace with him. He pointed out the various plants and grasses, naming them all, and telling her what would flower here in the spring, and what in the summer. He told her where the birds would nest, when their chicks would hatch and when they would fly. She listened not so much to the information, which she would never remember, but to the love of it in his voice.

It was a different world from London, but she began to see that it had a unique beauty, and perhaps if you loved a man deeply enough, and he loved you, then it could be a good land. Perhaps in Susannah's place she would have come here too. Jack had asked nothing of her, no sacrifice at all, except the forfeit of a little of the social position gained from her first husband. She still had the money she had inherited from him in trust for their son.

Jack had asked for no change in her, no sacrifice, not even an accommodation of awkward relatives. She realised with a chill of dismay that she did not even know his parents, or any of the friends he had had before they met. It was always her family they turned to. The belonging was all hers.

For the first time in their years together, she recognised a loss, and she was not certain how deep it was. With her acknowledgement of it entered a fear she had not known before. There were things she needed to learn, bitter or sweet. The ignorance was no longer acceptable.

When Emily arrived back at the house and went into the withdrawing room, she found to her surprise that Susannah had visitors. A rather portly older woman, with a handsome face and hair as rich as polished mahogany, was sitting in one of the armchairs, and standing to her side was a man at least twenty years younger, but with a very similar cast of features, only in him it was even more becoming, and his eyes were a finer hazel brown.

Susannah was sitting opposite them, dressed in blue and with her hair coiled up elegantly. She looked very pale, but she appeared attentive and cheerful. Emily could only imagine what the effort must cost her. She introduced the visitors as Mrs Flaherty and her son Brendan, explaining to them that Emily was her niece.

'Did you have a pleasant walk?' she asked.

'Yes, thank you,' Emily replied, sitting in one of the other chairs. 'I had not expected to find the shore so very beautiful. It is quite different from anything I know, much . . .' she searched for the right word.

'Wilder,' Brendan Flaherty offered for her. 'Like a beautiful animal, not savage intentionally, just doesn't know its own strength, and if you anger it, it will destroy you, because that is its nature.'

'You must excuse Brendan,' Mrs Flaherty apologised. 'He's overfanciful. He doesn't mean to alarm you.'

The colour rushed up Brendan's cheeks, but Emily was certain it was embarrassment for his mother's intervention, not for his own words.

'I find it a perfect description,' Emily smiled to take the

correction out of her words. 'I think it was the power of it I found beautiful, and in a way the delicacy. There were still some tiny wildflowers there, even at this time of the year.'

'Glad you saw them today,' Mrs Flaherty said. 'The storm will finish them. No idea how much sand it will put on top of everything. And weed, of course.'

Emily could think of no adequate reply. The look of bleakness in Mrs Flaherty's face made it impossible to be light about it.

'I met Mrs O'Donnell at the shop,' she said instead, 'and posted my letters. And then on the way back I walked a little way with a most interesting man, a Mr Yorke, who told me some stories about the village, and the area in general.'

Brendan smiled. 'He would. He's our local historian, sort of keeper of the collective spirit of the place. And something of a poet.'

Mrs Flaherty forced a smile as well. 'Takes a bit of liberty,' she added. 'A good bit of myth thrown in with his history.'

'True enough at heart, if not in every detail,' Brendan said to Emily.

'You're too generous,' his mother's voice was sharp. 'Some of what is passed around as history is just malicious. Idle tongues with nothing better to do.'

'There was nothing unpleasant,' Emily said quickly, although that was a slight stretch of the truth. 'Just old tales.'

'That's a surprise,' Mrs Flaherty responded disbelievingly. She glanced at Brendan, then back to Emily. 'I'm afraid we are a small village. We all know each other rather too well.' She rose to her feet stiffly. 'But I hope you'll enjoy yourself here. You're most welcome. We're all glad that Susannah has family to spend Christmas with her.' She made herself smile, and it lightened her face until one could see an echo of the young woman she had once been, fresh, full of hope, and almost beautiful.

'I'm sure I shall, Mrs Flaherty, but thank you for your good wishes.'

Brendan bade her goodbye as well, holding her gaze for a moment longer as if he would say something else, but when his mother looked at him urgently, he changed his mind.

Emily had a sharp image of Mrs Flaherty taking Brendan's arm, gripping it, not as if she needed his support but as if she dared not let him go.

When the door was closed and they were back inside, Emily looked more closely at Susannah.

'It's a good day,' Susannah assured her. 'I slept well. Did you really like the shore?'

'Yes, I did.' Emily was pleased to be honest. She had a sudden conviction that Hugo had loved it, and it mattered to Susannah that Emily could see its beauty also. 'And Mr Yorke didn't say anything except a little history of the Flahertys long ago,' she added.

Susannah lifted a hand in dismissal. 'Oh, don't take any notice of Mrs Flaherty. Her husband was a colourful character, but no real harm in him. At least that's what I choose to think, but I'm glad I wasn't married to him all the same. She adored him, but I think her memory must be a little kinder than the facts bear out. He was too handsome for his own good – or for hers.'

'I can believe it,' Emily agreed with a smile, thinking of Brendan walking away down the path with his easy stride.

Susannah understood her instantly. 'Oh, yes, Brendan too. Naturally he took advantage of it, and she spoiled him, in his father's memory, I think.'

'Did she remarry?' Emily asked.

Susannah's eyebrows shot up. 'Colleen Flaherty? Good heavens, no! As far as she's concerned, no one could fill Seamus's shoes. Not that I think anyone tried! Too busy guarding Brendan from what she saw as his father's weaknesses. Mostly women, the drink, and an overdose of imagination, so I gather. She's terrified Brendan'll go the same way. I don't think she's doing him a kindness, but it wouldn't help to say so.'

'And will he go the same way?' Emily asked.

Susannah looked at her, for a moment her eyes frank, almost probing, then she turned away. 'Maybe, but I hope not. From what Hugo used to say, Seamus Flaherty was a nightmare to live with. People with that kind of charm can jerk you up and down like a puppet on the end of a string. Sooner or later the string will break. Are you ready for lunch? You must be hungry after your walk.'

'Yes, I am. I'll make lunch, if you like?'

'Maggie was here and it's all done,' Susannah replied.

'Really?' Emily gestured towards the window. 'In spite of the storm?' She smiled.

'It'll come, Emily.' Susannah shuddered, her whole body closing in on itself as if she had wrapped her arms around it. 'Maybe tonight.'

By dusk the wind was very definitely rising again, and with a different sound from before. The keening was higher, a more dangerous edge to it. Darkness came very early and Emily noticed as she put things away after dinner that there were cold places in the house. In spite of all the windows being closed, somehow the air from outside found its way in. There seemed to be no lull between the gusts, as though nothing could rest any more.

The curtains were drawn closed, but Susannah kept looking towards the windows. There was no rain to hear, just the wind and occasionally the sudden hard bang as a twig hit the glass.

They were both happy to go to bed early.

'Perhaps by morning it will have blown itself out,' Emily said hopefully.

Susannah turned a white face towards her, eyes filled with fear. 'No, it won't,' she said quietly, the wind almost drowning her words. 'Not yet. Maybe not ever.'

Emily's common sense wanted to tell her that that was stupid, but she knew it would not help. Whatever Susannah was talking about, it was something far more than the wind.

Perhaps it was whatever she was really afraid of, and the reason she had wanted Emily here.

Emily thought as she undressed that in London Jack would be at the theatre, possibly enjoying the interval, laughing with their friends at the play, swapping gossip. Or would he not have gone without her? It wouldn't be the same, would it?

Surprisingly, she went to sleep fairly quickly, but she woke with a jolt. She had no idea what time it was, except that she was in total darkness. She could see nothing whatever. The wind had risen to a high, constant scream.

Then it came – a flare of lightning so vivid that it lit the room even through the drawn curtains. The thunder was all but instantaneous, crashing round and round, as if it came from all directions.

For a moment she lay motionless. The lightning blazed again, a brief, spectral glare, almost shadowless, then it was gone and there was only the roaring of thunder and shrill scream of the wind.

She threw the covers off and, picking up a shawl from the chair, went to the window. She pulled the curtains back but the darkness was impenetrable. The noise was demonic, louder without the muffling of the curtains. This was ridiculous; she would have seen as much if she had stayed in bed with the covers over her head, like a child.

Then the lightning struck again, and showed her a world in torment. The few trees in the garden were thrashing wildly, broken twigs flying. The sky was filled with roiling clouds so low they closed in as if to settle on the earth. But it was the sea that held her eyes. In the glare it seethed white with spume, heaving as if trying to break its bounds and rise to consume the land. The howl of it could be heard even above the wind.

Then the darkness returned in as if she had been blinded. She could not see even the glass inches from her face. She was cold. There was nothing to do, nothing to achieve, and yet she stood on the spot as if she were fixed to it.

The lightning flared again, at almost the same moment as the thunder, sheets of colourless light across the sky, then forks like stab wounds from heaven to the sea. And there, quite clearly out in the bay, was a ship struggling from the north, battered and overwhelmed, trying to make its way around the headland to Galway. It was going to fail. Emily knew that as surely as if it had already happened. The sea was going to devour it.

She felt almost obscene, standing here in the safety of the house, watching while people were destroyed in front of her. But neither could she simply turn round and go back to bed, even if what she had seen were a dream and would all have vanished in the morning. They would be dying, choking in the water while she lay there warm and safe.

It was probably pointless to waken Susannah, as if Emily were a child who could not cope with a nightmare alone, and yet she did not hesitate. She tied the shawl more tightly around her and went along the corridor with a candle in her hand.

She knocked on Susannah's bedroom door, prepared to go in if she were not answered.

She knocked again, harder, more urgently. She heard Susannah's voice and opened the door.

Susannah sat up slowly, her face pale, her long hair tousled. In the yellow light of the flame she looked almost young again, almost well.

'Did the storm disturb you?' she asked quietly. 'You don't need to worry; the house has withstood many like this before.'

'It's not for me,' Emily closed the bedroom door behind her, a tacit signal she did not mean to leave. 'There's a ship out in the bay, in terrible trouble. I suppose there's nothing we can do, but I have to be sure.' She sounded ridiculous. Of course there was nothing. She simply did not want to watch its sinking alone.

The horror in Susannah's eyes was worse than anything Emily could have imagined.

'Susannah! Is there somebody you know on it?' she went forward quickly and grasped Susannah's hands on the counterpane. They were stiff and cold.

'No,' Susannah replied hoarsely. 'I don't think so. But that hardly makes it different, does it? Don't we all know each other, when it matters?'

There was no answer. They stood side by side at the window staring into the darkness, then as the lightning came again, a searing flash, it left an imprint on the eyes of a ship floundering in cavernous waves, hurled one way and then another, struggling to keep bow to the wind. As soon as they were tossed sideways they would be rolled over, pummelled to pieces and sucked downwards for ever. The sailors must know that, just as Emily did. The two women were watching something inevitable, and yet Emily found her body rigid with the effort of hope that somehow it would not be so.

She stood closer to Susannah, touching her. Susannah took her hand, gripping it. The ship was still afloat, battling south towards the point. Once it was out of sight, would anyone ever know what had happened to them?

As if reading Emily's thoughts, Susannah said, 'They're probably bound for Galway, but they might take shelter in Cashel, just beyond the headland. It's a big bay, complicated. There's plenty of calm water, whichever way the wind's coming.'

'Is it often like this?' Emily asked, appalled at the thought. Susannah did not answer.

'Is it?'

'Once before . . .' Susannah began, then drew in her breath in a gasp of pain so fierce Emily all but felt it herself as Susannah's fingers clenched around hers, bruising the bones.

Emily stared out into the pitch-darkness, and then the lightning burned again, and the ship was gone. She saw it in a moment of hideous clarity, just the mast above the seething water.

Susannah turned back to the room. 'I must go and tell

Fergal O'Bannion. He'll get the rest of the men of the village out. Someone . . . may be washed ashore. We'll need to . . .'

'I'll go.' Emily put her hand on Susannah's arm, holding her back. 'I know where he lives.'

'You'll never see your way . . .' Susannah began.

'I'll take a lantern. Anyway, does it really matter if I get the right house? If I wake someone else, they'll get Fergal. Can we do anything more than give them a decent burial?'

Susannah's voice was a whisper forced between her lips. 'Someone could be alive. It has happened before . . .'

'I'll go and get Fergal O'Bannion,' Emily said. 'Please keep warm. I don't suppose you can go back to sleep, but rest.'

Susannah nodded. 'Hurry.'

Emily went back to her room and dressed as quickly as she could, then took a lantern from the hall and went out of the front door. Suddenly she was in the middle of a maelstrom. The wind shrieked and howled like a chorus of mad things. In the lightning she could see trees breaking as if they were plywood. Then the darkness was absolute again, until she raised the lantern, shining a weak yellow shaft in front of her.

She went forward, picking her way on the unfamiliar path, having to lean all her weight against the gate to force it open. On the road she stumbled and felt a moment of terror that she would fall and smash the lantern, perhaps cut herself. Then she would be utterly lost.

'Stupid!' she said aloud, although she could not hear her

own words in the bedlam of the elements. 'Don't be so feeble!' she snapped at herself. She was on dry land. All she had to do was keep her feet, and walk. There were people out there being swallowed by the sea.

She increased her pace, holding the lantern as high as she could until her arm ached and she was weaving around in the road as the wind knocked her off her path, then relented suddenly and left her pushing against nothing.

She was gasping for breath as she finally staggered to the doorway of the first house she came to. She really didn't care whether it was Fergal O'Bannion's or not. She banged many times, and no one answered. She backed away and found several pebbles from the garden and threw them up at the largest window. If she broke it she would apologise, even pay for it. But she would have smashed every window in the house if it gave her even a chance of helping any of those men out there in the bay.

She flung them hard and heard them clatter; the last one cracked ominously.

A few moments later the door opened and she saw Fergal's startled face and rumpled hair. He recognised Emily immediately. 'Is Mrs Ross worse?' he asked hoarsely.

'No. No, there's a ship gone down in the bay,' Emily gasped. 'She said you'd know what to do, in case there were any survivors.'

A sudden fear came into his face and he stood motionless in the doorway.

'Do you?' Her voice cracked in panic.

He looked as if she had struck him. 'Yes. I'll get Maggie to get the others. I'll set out for the shore, in case . . .' He did not finish the sentence.

'Can anyone really survive this?' she asked him.

He did not answer, but retreated into the house, leaving the door wide for her to follow. A few moments later he came down the stairs again fully dressed, Maggie behind him.

'I'll fetch everyone I can,' she said, after briefly acknowledging Emily. 'You go to the shore. I'll get blankets and whiskey and we'll bring them. Go!'

White faced, he picked up a lantern and stepped out into the night.

Emily looked at Maggie.

'Come with me,' Maggie said without hesitation. 'We'll get who else we can.' She lit another lantern, pulled her shawl around her and went out also.

Together they struggled along the road, although it would not be as bad here as on the shore. Maggie pointed to one house and told Emily the name of the people in it, while she went one further along. One by one, shouting and banging, occasionally throwing more stones, they raised nearly a dozen men to go down along the beach, and as many women to get whiskey and blankets, and cans of stew off the stove and chunks of bread.

'Could be a long night,' Maggie said drily, her face bleak, eyes filled with fear and pity. In twos and threes they made their way across the hummocks of grass and sand. Emily was confused by how many houses they had missed out. 'Would they not come?' she asked, having to shout above the clamour. 'Surely anyone would help when people are drowning? Do you want me to go back and try?'

'No.' Maggie reached out and took her arm, as if to force her forward, into the wind. They were closer to the water now and could hear the deep roar of it like a great beast.

'But—' Emily began.

'They're empty,' Maggie shouted back. 'Gone.'

'All of them?' That was impossible. She was speaking of almost half the village. Then Emily remembered Father Tyndale's apology for the sparseness of the place now, and a great hollowness opened up as if at her feet. The village was dying. That was what he had meant.

Another flare of lightning burned across the sky and she saw the enormity of the sea far closer than she had imagined. The power and savagery of it was terrifying, but it was also beautiful. She felt a kind of bereavement when the flare died and again she could see nothing but the bobbing yellow lanterns, the fold of a skirt, a leg of trouser, and a swaying movement of sand and grass below. Several of the men had great lengths of rope, she wondered what for.

They were strung out along the beach, some closer to the white rage of the water than she could bear to look at. What could they do? The strongest boat ever built could not put to sea in this. They would be smashed, overturned and dragged under before they were fifty yards out. That would help no one.

She looked at Maggie.

Maggie's face was set towards the sea, but even in the wavering gleam of the lantern Emily could see the fear in her, the wide eyes, the tight muscles of her jaw, the quick breathing.

She looked away, along the shore, and saw in the next flash the large figure of Father Tyndale, the furthest man along the line.

'I'll take the Father some bread and whiskey,' Emily offered. 'Or does he not . . . ?'

Maggie forced a smile. 'Oh, he wouldn't mind in the least,' she assured her. 'He gets as much cold in his bones as anyone else.'

With a brief smile Emily set out leaning into the wind, pushed and pulled by it until she felt bruised, her feet dragging in the fine sand, the noise deafening her. She judged where she was by the slope of the shore, and every now and then climbed a little higher as the wind carried the spray and she was drenched. The thunder was swallowed up by the noise of the waves, but every lightning flare lit up the whole shore with a ghastly, spectral clarity.

She reached Father Tyndale, shouting to him just as another huge wave roared in and she was completely inaudible. She held out the whiskey and the packet of bread. He smiled at her and accepted it, gulping down the spirits and shuddering as the fire of it hit his throat. He undid the parcel of bread and ate it hungrily, ignoring the sea spray and wind-driven rain that must have soaked it. Even in the smothering darkness in between the lightning flares, he never seemed to have moved his gaze from the sea.

Emily looked back the way she had come, seeing the string of lanterns, each steady as if they were gripped hard. No one appeared to move. She had no idea what time it was, or how long since she had woken and seen the ship.

Did this happen every winter? Was that why they had spoken of the storm with such dread, nights waiting for the sea to regurgitate its dead? Perhaps people from the surrounding villages, whom they knew?

The wind had not abated at all, but now there were gaps between the lightning and the thunder that followed it. Very slowly the storm was passing.

Then, after three flashes of sheet lightning, two of the lanterns were raised high in the air and swung in some kind of a signal. Father Tyndale gripped Emily's arm and pulled her along as he started to run, floundering in the sand. She scrambled after him, hanging on to her lantern.

By the time they reached the spot where the signal had been given, four men were already roped together and the leading one was fighting his way against the waves deeper into the sea, battered, pummelled, but each flare of lightning showed him further out.

It seemed an endless wait but in fact it was probably little more then ten minutes before the others started heaving on the rope and backing further up the beach onto the weed-laced shore. The women huddled together, lanterns making a pool of light on the sodden men as one by one they were hauled ashore, exhausted, stumbling to their knees before gasping, and turning back to help those still behind them.

The last man, Brendan Flaherty, was carrying a body in his arms. Others reached forward to help him, and he staggered up the sand to lay it gently beyond the sea's reach. Father Tyndale clasped his shoulder and shouted something, lost in the wind and roar of the water, then bent to the body.

Emily looked at the villagers' faces as they stood in a half-circle, the yellow flares of the lanterns under-lighting their features, hair wet and wind whipped, eyes dark. There was pity in their knowledge of death and loss, but more than anything else she was touched again by the drenching sense of fear.

She looked down at the body. It was that of a young man, in his late twenties. His skin was ashen white, a little blue around the eye sockets and lips. His hair looked black in this lantern light, and it clung to his head, straggling across his brow. He was quite tall, probably slender under the seaman's jacket and rough trousers. Above all, he was handsome. It was a dreamer's face, a man with a world inside his head.

Emily wanted to ask if he was dead, against her will imagining how it had happened, but she dreaded the answer. She looked one by one at the ring of faces around her. They were motionless, gripped by pity, and more than that, by horror.

'Do you know him?' Emily asked, a sudden lull in the wind making it seem as if she were shouting at them.

'No,' they answered. 'No . . .'

And yet she was certain that they were looking at something they had half expected to see. There was no surprise in them at all, no puzzlement, just a dreadful certainty.

'Is he dead?' she asked Father Tyndale.

'No,' Father Tyndale answered. 'Here, Fergal, help me get him up on my shoulder, and I'll carry him to Susannah's. We'll need to get him warm and dry. Maggie, will you stay with him? And Mrs Radley, no doubt?'

'Yes, of course,' Emily agreed. 'We're by far the closest, and we have plenty of room.'

When they reached the house Susannah must have been up and looking out of the window, because she opened the door before anyone knocked. The young man was carried upstairs, awkwardly, booted feet scraping and numb hands knocking against the banisters. He was laid on the floor and the women asked to leave. Susannah had already put out a nightshirt, presumably one of Hugo's she had kept. Emily wondered if she had kept all his clothes.

There were no sheets on the bed, only blankets. 'Shall I—' Emily began.

'Blankets are warmer,' Susannah cut across her. 'Sheets later, when the blood's flowing again.' She looked down at the young man's face and there was sadness in her own, and fear, as if something long dreaded had happened at last.

Then they excused themselves and went to get bowls of hot soup for the men, and all the dry woollens and socks they could find. The men would all have to go back again. There could be more people washed up, dead or alive.

The rest of the night Emily spent taking turns with Maggie O'Bannion to watch the young man, rub his hands and feet, change the oven-warmed stones wrapped in cloths in the bed, and watch him to see any signs of returning consciousness. No one had any idea how much water he had swallowed, and there were dark bruises and abrasions on his chest, legs and shoulders, as if he had been driven up against the wreckage again and again.

'I can't manage two of you to nurse,' Maggie said tartly when Susannah tried to argue about staying to help. 'Nor can Mrs Radley. She's come to visit you, not to watch you waste yourself away to no purpose.'

Susannah obeyed with a bleak smile, her eyes meeting Emily's before she turned away.

'Maybe I shouldn't have spoke harshly to her,' Maggie looked guilty. 'But she's—'

'I know,' Emily responded. 'You did the right thing.'

Maggie smiled briefly, and bent to wrap some hot stones in flannel. But Emily had seen the tension in her, the tight shoulders and the quick averting of her eyes.

Later, towards six o'clock in the morning, the young man

still had not stirred, but he was definitely warmer and his pulse quite strong. It was not dawn yet and Emily set out to take more whiskey and hot meals down to the men waiting on the shore, watching for the sea to yield more bodies.

She found them easily by the yellow light of their lanterns. The waves were crashing like huge avalanches of water, breaking on the sand and roaring higher and higher as the tide swept in. They hissed out long white tongues of foam right into the grass, as if trying to tear out its roots.

Emily went first to Father Tyndale. In the yellow lantern light he looked exhausted, his large frame somehow hunch shouldered, his face bleak.

'Ah, thank you, Mrs Radley.' He accepted the hot drink, but took of it sparingly to leave plenty for the others. 'It's a hard night.' He did not look at her as he spoke but out over the ocean. 'Has he woken yet?'

'No, Father. But he looks better.'

'Ah.'

She searched his expression, but the wavering light was deceptive and she could read nothing. He handed the flask back, and she took it to Brendan Flaherty, then Fergal O'Bannion, and on around the rest of them. Finally she walked back towards the house, so tired it was hard to keep upright against the wind. She thought of Jack at home in bed in London. How much was he missing her? Had he even the remotest idea what he had asked of her, he would not have done it – would he?

She slept for perhaps an hour. It seemed almost impossible to climb out of the depths of unconsciousness when Maggie shook her and spoke her name. At first Emily could not even remember where she was.

'He's awake,' Maggie said quietly. 'I'm going to get him something to eat. Perhaps you'd sit with him. He seems a bit distressed.'

'Of course.' Emily realised she still had most of her clothes on, and she was stiff as if she had walked miles. Then she remembered the storm. The wind was howling and keening in the eaves, but less violently than before. 'Did he say anything? Did you tell him he was the only one?' she asked.

'Not yet. I'm not sure how he'll take it.' Maggie looked guilty, and Emily knew she was afraid to do it. She shivered and reached for her shawl. In all that had happened last night, she had not thought to add peat to the fire, and it had gone out. The air was chill.

She went to the room where the young man was, knocked, and went in without waiting for an answer. He was lying propped against the pillows, his face still ashen, eyes dark and hollow. She walked over and stood beside him.

'Maggie's gone to get you something to eat,' she said. 'My name is Emily. What is yours?'

He thought for several moments, blinking solemnly. 'Daniel,' he said at last.

'Daniel who?'

He shook his head and winced as though it hurt. 'I don't

know. All I can remember is the water all around me. And men calling out, fighting, to . . . to stay alive. Where are they?'

'I don't know,' she said honestly. 'I'm sorry, but you were the only one we found. We stayed on the beach all night, but no one else was washed up.'

'They all drowned?' he said slowly.

'I'm afraid it seems so.'

'All of them.' There was deep pain in his face and his voice was very quiet. 'I can't remember how many there were. Five or six, I think.' He looked at her. 'I can't even think of the ship's name.'

'I expect it'll come back to you. Give yourself a little time. Do you hurt anywhere?'

He smiled with a grim humour. 'Everywhere, as if I'd taken the beating of my life. But it'll pass.' He closed his eyes, and when he opened them again they were full of tears. 'I'm alive.' He reached out his hands, strong and slender, and clasped them over the softness of the quilt, digging into its warmth.

Maggie came in with a dish of porridge and milk. 'Let me help you with this,' she offered. 'I dare say it's long enough since you had anything inside you.' She sat down and held the bowl in her hands, offering him the spoon. Emily saw that in spite of the fact that she was smiling, her knuckles were white.

Daniel looked at her and clasped the spoon. Slowly he

filled it and raised it to his mouth. He swallowed, then took some more.

Maggie continued to watch him but her eyes were concentrated on something far away, as if she had no need to focus any more to know what she would see. She still gripped the dish tightly and Emily watched her chest rise and fall and the pulse beat in her throat.

Emily went back to bed briefly, this time falling asleep immediately. She woke to find Susannah beside her with a tray of tea and two slices of toast. She set it down on the small table and drew the curtains wide. The wind was moaning and rattling, but there were large patches of blue in the sky.

'I sent Maggie home for a little sleep,' Susannah said with a smile as she poured the tea, a cup for each of them. 'The toast is for you,' she added. 'Daniel has eaten some more, and gone back to sleep again, but when I looked in on him he was disturbed. I'm sure he must be having nightmares.'

'I imagine he will for years.' Emily sipped her tea and picked up a slice of the crisp hot-buttered toast. 'Now I see why everyone so dreaded the storm.'

Susannah looked up quickly, then smiled and said nothing.

'Do they come like this often?' Emily went on.

Susannah turned away. 'No, not often at all. Do you feel well enough to go to the store and get some more food? There are a few things we will need, with an extra person here.'

'Of course,' Emily agreed. 'But he won't stay long, will he?'

'I don't know. Do you mind?'

'Of course not.'

But later, as she was walking along the sea front towards the village, Emily wondered why Susannah had thought the young man would stay. Surely as soon as he had rested sufficiently, he would want to be on his way to Galway, to contact his family, and the people who owned his ship. His memory would return with a little more rest, and he would be eager to leave.

She came over the slight rise towards the shore and looked out at the troubled sea, wracks of white spume spread across it, the waves, uncrested now in the falling wind, but still mountainous, roaring far up the shore and into the grass with frightening speed, gouging out the sand, consuming it into itself. It was the shadowless grey of molten lead, and it looked as solid.

At the shop she found Mary O'Donnell and the woman who had introduced herself as Kathleen. They stopped talking the moment Emily walked in.

'How are you, then?' Kathleen asked with a smile, as if now that Emily had endured the storm she was part of the village.

Mary gave her a quick, almost guarded look, then as if it had been only a trick of the light, she turned to Emily also. 'You must be tired, after last night. How's the young sailor, poor soul?'

'Exhausted,' Emily replied. 'But he had some breakfast,

and I expect by tomorrow he'll be recovering well. At least physically, of course. He'll be a long time before he forgets the fear, and the grief.'

'So he's not badly hurt, then?' Kathleen asked.

'Bruised, so far as I know,' Emily told her.

'And who is he?' Mary said softly.

There was a sudden silence in the shop. Mr Yorke was in the doorway, but he stood motionless. He looked at Kathleen, then at Mary. Neither of them looked at him.

'Daniel,' Emily replied. 'He seems to have forgotten the rest of his name, just for the moment.'

The jar of pickles in Mary O'Donnell's hands slipped and fell to the floor, bursting open in splintered glass. No one moved.

Mr Yorke came in the door and walked over to it. 'Can I help you?' he offered.

Mary came to life. 'Oh! How stupid. I'm so sorry.' She bent to help Mr Yorke, bumping into him in her fluster. 'What a mess!'

Emily waited; there was nothing she could do to help. When the mess was all swept and mopped up, the pickle and broken glass were put in the bin, and there was no more to mark the accident than a wet patch on the floor, and a smell of vinegar in the air. Mary filled Emily's list for her and put it all in her bag. No one mentioned the young man from the sea again. Emily thanked them and went out into the wind. She looked back once, and saw them standing together, staring after her, faces white.

She walked back along the edge of the shore. The tide was receding and there was a strip of hard, wet sand, here and there strewn with weed torn from the bottom of the ocean and thrown there by the waves. She saw pieces of wood, broken, jagged ended, and found herself cold inside. She did not know if they were from the ship that had gone down, but they were from something man-made that had been broken and drowned. She knew there were no more bodies. Either they had been carried out to sea and lost for ever, or they were cast up on some other shore, perhaps the rocks out by the point. She could not bear to think of them battered there, torn apart and exposed.

In spite of the wild, clean air, the sunlight slanting through the clouds, she felt a sense of desolation settle over her, like a chill in the bones.

She did not hear the steps behind her. The sand was soft, and the sound of the waves consumed everything else.

'Good morning, Mrs Radley.'

She stopped and twisted round, clasping the bag closer to her. Father Tyndale was only a couple of yards away, hatless, the wind blowing his hair and making his dark jacket flap like the wings of a wounded crow.

'Good morning, Father,' she said with a sense of relief that surprised her. Who had she been expecting? 'You . . . you haven't found anyone else, have you?'

'No, I'm afraid not.' His face was sad, as if he too were bruised.

'Do you think they could have survived? Perhaps the ship didn't go down? Maybe Daniel was washed overboard?' she suggested.

'Perhaps.' There was no belief in his voice. 'Can I carry your shopping for you?' He reached out for it and since it was heavy, she was happy enough to pass it to him.

'How is Susannah this morning?' he asked. There was more than concern in his face – there was fear. 'And Maggie O'Bannion – is she all right?'

'Yes, of course she is. We're all tired, and grieved for the loss of life, but no one is otherwise worse.'

He did not answer; in fact he did not even acknowledge that he had heard her.

She was about to repeat it more vehemently, then she realised that he was asking with profound anxiety, the undercurrent of which she had felt increasingly since the wind first started rising. He was not asking about health or tiredness, he was looking for something of the heart that battled against fear.

'Do you know the young man who was washed ashore, Father Tyndale?' she asked.

He stopped abruptly.

'His name is Daniel,' she added. 'He doesn't seem to remember anything more. Do you know him?'

He stood staring at her, buffeted by the wind, his face a mask of unhappiness. 'No, Mrs Radley, I have no idea who he is, or why he has come here.' He did not look at her.

'He didn't come here, Father,' she corrected him. 'The storm brought him. Who is he?'

'I've told you, I have no idea,' he repeated.

It was an odd choice of words, a total denial, not merely the ordinary claim of ignorance she had expected. Something was wrong in the village. It was dying in more than numbers. There was a fear in the air that had nothing to do with the storm. That had been and gone now, but the darkness remained.

'Perhaps I should ask you what Daniel means to these people, Father,' Emily said suddenly. 'I'm the stranger here. Everyone seems to know something that I don't.'

'Daniel, is it?' he mused, and a lull in the wind made his voice seem loud.

'So he says. You sound surprised. Do you know him as something else?' She heard the harshness of her words, the edge of her own fear showing through.

'I don't know him at all, Mrs Radley,' he repeated, but he did not look at her, and the misery in his genial face deepened.

She put her hand on his arm, holding on to him hard, obliging him either to stop, or very deliberately to shake her off, and he was too well mannered to do that. He stopped in front of her.

'What is it, Father Tyndale?' she asked. 'It's the storm and Daniel, and something else. Everybody's afraid, as if they knew there was going to be a ship go down. What's wrong with the village? What is it that Susannah really wants me here for? And don't say it's family at Christmas. Susannah was estranged from the family. Her love was Hugo Ross, and perhaps this place and these people. This is where she was happiest in her life. She wants me here for something else. What is it?'

His face filled with pity. 'I know, my dear, but she is asking more than you can do, more than anyone can.'

She tightened her fingers on his arm. 'What, Father? I can't even try if I don't know what it is?'

He gave a deep sigh. 'Seven years ago there was another storm, like this one. Another ship was lost out in the bay; it too was trying to beat its way round to Galway. That night too, there was just one survivor, a young man called Connor Riordan. He was washed ashore half dead, and we took him in and nursed him. It was this time of the year, a couple of weeks before Christmas.' He blinked hard, as if the wind were in his eyes, except that he had his back to it.

'Yes?' Emily prompted. 'What happened to him?'

'The weather was very bad,' Father Tyndale went on, speaking now as if to himself as much as to her. 'He was a good-looking young man, not unlike this one. Black hair, dark eyes, something of the dreamer in him. Very quick, he was, interested in everything. And he could sing – oh, he could sing. Sad songs, all on the half-note, the half-beat. Gave it a kind of haunting sound. He made friends. Everyone liked him – to begin with.'

Emily felt a chill, but she did not interrupt him.

'He asked a lot of questions,' Father Tyndale went on, his voice lower. 'Deep questions, that made you think of morality and belief, and just who and what you really were. That's not always a comfortable thing to do.' He looked up at the sky and the shredded clouds streaming across it. 'He disturbed both dreams and demons. Made people face dark things they weren't ready for.'

'And then he left?' she asked, trying to read the tragedy in his face. 'Why? Surely that wasn't a bad thing? He went back home, then probably out in another ship.'

'No,' Father Tyndale said so quietly the wind all but swallowed his words. 'No, he never left.'

She crushed on the fear rising inside her. 'What do you mean? He's still here?'

'In a manner of speaking.'

'Manner . . . what kind of manner?' Now that she had asked, she did not want to know. But it was too late.

'Over there.' He lifted his hand. 'Out towards the point, his body's buried. We'll never forget him. We've tried, and we can't.'

'His family didn't . . . didn't come and take his body?'

'No one knew he was here,' Father Tyndale said simply. 'He came from the sea one night when every other soul in his ship was lost. It was winter, and the wind and rain were hard. No one from outside the village came here during those weeks, and we knew nothing of him except his name.'

The cold was enlarging inside her, ugly and painful. 'How did he die, Father?'

'He drowned,' he replied, and there was a look on his face as if he were admitting to something so terrible he could not force himself to say it aloud.

There was only one thought in Emily's mind, but she too would not say it. Connor Riordan had been murdered. The village knew it, and the secret had been poisoning them all these years.

'Who?' she said softly.

He could not have heard her voice above the wind in the grass. He read her lips, and her mind. It was the one thing anyone would ask.

'I don't know,' he said helplessly. 'I'm the spiritual father of these people. I'm supposed to love them and keep them, comfort their griefs and heal their wounds, and absolve their sins. And I don't know!' His voice dropped until it was hoarse, painful to hear. 'I've asked myself every night since then, how can I have been in the presence of such passion and such darkness, and not know it?'

Emily ached to be able to answer him. She knew the subtle and terrible twists of murder, and how often nothing is what it seems to be. Long ago her own eldest sister had been a victim, and yet when the truth was known, she had felt more pity than rage for the one so tormented that they had killed again and again, driven by an inner pain no one else could touch.

'We don't,' she said gently, at last letting go of Father

Tyndale's arm. 'I knew someone quite well, once, who killed many times. And when in the end everything was plain, I understood.'

'But these are my people!' he protested, his voice trembling. 'I hear their confessions. I, above all, know their loves and hates, their fears and their dreams. How can I listen to them, and yet have no idea who has done this? Whatever it was, they could have come to me, they should have known they could!' He spread his hands. 'I didn't save Connor's life, and infinitely worse than that, I didn't save the soul of whoever killed him. Or those who are even now protecting him. The whole village is dying because of it, and I am powerless. I don't have the faith or the strength to help.'

She could think of nothing to say that was not trite and would sound as if she had no understanding of his pain.

He looked down at the sand shifting and blowing about their feet. 'And now this new young man has come, like a revisiting of death, as if it were all going to happen again. And I am still useless.'

Emily hurt for him, for all of them. Now she understood what it was that Susannah wanted resolved before she died. Did she think Emily could do it because of the times she and Charlotte had involved themselves in Pitt's cases? They had found facts, but she had no idea how to detect from the beginning, understand what mattered and what didn't, and put everything in its right place to tell a story. Always a tragic story.

Hugo Ross had been alive when Connor Riordan had been here. What had he known? Was Susannah afraid that he had been involved somehow, shielding someone from the law because they were his own people? Or was she afraid that they would blame Hugo, once she was gone and could no longer protect his memory?

Emily wanted to help, with a fierceness that consumed and amazed her, but she had no idea how.

Father Tyndale saw it in her face. He shook his head. 'You can't, my dear. I told you that. Don't blame yourself. I have known these people all of their lives, and I don't know. You've come here just days ago from a foreign land – how could you?'

But that was no comfort to Emily as she unpacked the shopping on the kitchen table for Maggie to put away.

She went into the drawing room, to find Daniel up and dressed in clothes that were far too big for him, but at least were of the right length. They must have been Hugo Ross's, and one look at Susannah's face confirmed it to her.

'Thank you for your care, Mrs Radley,' Daniel said with a smile that gave him a sudden warmth and that kind of acute but gentle intelligence that comes with humour. 'I feel fine, except for a good many aches and some bruises a prizefighter would be proud of.' He shrugged. 'But I still can't remember much, except choking and freezing, and thinking I was going to die.'

'What did the other men call you?' Emily asked curiously.

He hesitated, racking his memory. 'Daniel, I suppose. That's all I can remember.'

'And them?' she pressed.

'There was a . . . a Joe, I think.' He frowned. 'There was a big man with a lot of tattoos. I think his name was Wat, or something like that. Are they all gone? Are you sure?'

'We don't know,' Susannah answered him. 'We waited all night, but no one else was washed up here. I'm sorry.' Her voice was gentle but her eyes searched his face. What was she looking for, traces of a lie? A memory of something else? Or did she see in him the ghost of Connor Riordan and the tragedy he awakened?

'What day is it?' Daniel asked suddenly, looking from Susannah to Emily, and back again.

'Saturday,' Emily replied.

'There must be a church here. I saw a priest. I'd like to go to Mass tomorrow. I need to thank God for my own deliverance and, more than that, I must pray for the souls of my friends. Perhaps God will grant me my memory back. No man should die so alone that his name is not said by those who survived.'

'Yes, of course,' Susannah said immediately. 'I'll take you. It isn't far.'

Emily clenched inside. 'Are you sure you are well enough?' She wanted to find any way, any excuse for her not to. It was natural that Daniel should wish to go and say Mass for his comrades – what decent man would not? He had almost certainly never heard of Connor Riordan, whose death had nothing to do with this storm, or this loss. But the village could see ghosts in his face, and one person at least would feel guilt.

'Yes, of course,' Susannah said a trifle sharply. 'We'll all feel better tomorrow.'

But in the morning Susannah was so weak that when she came into the kitchen she had to clutch at the back of a chair to keep from losing her balance and falling.

Emily leaped to her feet and caught her, steadying her with both arms and easing her to sit.

'I'm all right!' Susannah said weakly. 'I just need a little breakfast. Have you seen Daniel this morning?'

'Not yet, but I heard him up. Susannah, please go back to bed. You aren't well enough to walk to church. The wind is still strong.'

'I told you,' Susannah said sharply, 'I'll feel far better when I've had a cup of tea and something to eat—'

'Susannah,' Emily cut across her, commanding her attention, 'you can't go to church like this. It will embarrass everyone, mostly you. We should be there to thank God for Daniel's life, and to pay our respects to those who were lost, whoever they were.'

'Daniel can't go alone . . .' Susannah started.

'I'll go with him. The church can't be difficult to find.'

'You're not Catholic,' Susannah pointed out. There was a very slight smile in her eyes. 'I know you don't even approve, never mind believe.'

'Do *you*?' Emily asked. 'Or was it for Hugo?'

Susannah smiled ruefully. 'To begin with it was for Hugo. But afterwards, it was for myself.' Her voice dropped. 'Especially after Hugo died. I believed it because he had. It reminded me of all that he was.'

Emily felt an overwhelming sorrow for her. And she realised with a stab of ugly surprise that she knew Jack's politics in detail. She had helped him in all kinds of projects and battles and she was proud of what he had achieved. But she had no idea what his religious beliefs were. They both went to church on most Sundays, but so did everyone else. They had never discussed why.

'This would be a good time for me to look,' she said aloud. 'Ignorance is not a reason for disbelieving anything.'

'But you don't know—'

'Why you want to go?' Emily finished for her. 'Yes I do. Father Tyndale told me.'

Susannah looked confused. 'Told you what? About the church?'

'No, about Connor Riordan – seven years ago.'

'Oh! He told you . . .'

'Isn't that why you wanted me here?' Emily persisted. 'To help you look for the truth?'

'I didn't know there was going to be a storm this bad,' Susannah said quietly, her face ashen. 'And no one could have known Daniel would come.'

'Of course not. But you still needed to know who killed

Connor and be sure in your own heart that Hugo was not protecting someone he cared for out of loyalty, or pity.'

Susannah was so pale it seemed as if there could be no blood under her skin. Emily felt pierced by guilt, but to retreat now would leave the matter torn open, yet still unresolved, worse than if she had not touched it.

'I'll take Daniel to church,' she repeated. 'I'll watch, and tell you what happens. Don't worry about luncheon. There's cold meat, and a few vegetables will take no time at all.'

She walked along the road beside Daniel, who was dressed in one of Hugo's better suits. It was too large for him, but he made no comment on it except to smile at himself, and touch the texture of the cloth with appreciation.

They spoke little. Daniel was still weak and bruised, and it took him both effort and self-discipline to move with the appearance of ease, and to keep up a reasonable pace against the wind.

Emily thought of her family at home, and wondered with a touch of self-mockery what Jack would think if he could see her walking briskly along a rough road in a village she did not know, accompanying a young man washed up by the sea. And to crown it all, she was taking him to a Catholic church. It could hardly be what he had intended when he had coerced her into leaving her children at Christmas!

Then as the wind buffeted her and blew her skirts, almost knocking her off balance, she thought of Susannah and her marriage to Hugo Ross, and wondered if her father had ever met Hugo, or if he had shut Susannah out without knowing what she had chosen instead of a conventional marriage he would have approved of, and she would have hated. She had done that once, obediently, in her youth. The death of her first husband had freed her. She had married Hugo for love. Losing him took the heart from her life. She walked on alone towards that horizon beyond which they would be together again.

Emily and Daniel reached the low stone church and went inside. It was only half full, as if it had been built for a far larger congregation. She saw a startled look on Father Tyndale's face, and that was possibly what caused several other people to turn and stare as she and Daniel found seats towards the back. She recognised the women from the shop, sitting with men and children who must be their families. She also saw Fergal and Maggie O'Bannion, and Mrs Flaherty with Brendan beside her, head bent. She knew him only from his thick, curling hair. She thought the straggling grey head belonged to Padraic Yorke.

Beside her Daniel said nothing but kneeled slowly in silent prayer. She wondered if any memory at all had come back to him of the shipmates he had lost, and she ached for his confusion and what must be a consuming loneliness.

She found the service alien, and seemed always to be a step behind everyone else, and yet reluctantly she had to admit there was a beauty in it, and a strange half familiarity, as if once she might have known it. Watching Father Tyndale solemnly, almost mystically, blessing the bread and the wine, she saw him in a different light, far more than a decent man doing what he could for his neighbours. For that short space he was the shepherd of his people, and she saw the pain in his face with a dreadful clarity.

But she was here to observe for Susannah. While the service was continuing she could watch only from behind. Fergal and Maggie O'Bannion sat very close to each other, he constantly adjusting his weight so that his arm touched hers, she leaning away from him whenever she could, as though she felt crowded. Did they feel as apart as that suggested?

Mrs Flaherty had a hand quite openly on Brendan's arm, and once Emily saw him deliberately shake it off, only for his mother to replace it a few moments later. Emily glanced sideways at Daniel, and saw that he had noticed also. Was that chance? Looking at his solemn face, with its huge, hollow eyes and sensitive mouth, all humour gone from it now, he seemed to be studying the people as much as she was.

After the service it was the same. She saw Fergal and Maggie standing side by side talking to Father Tyndale, looking as if they were physically so close only by accident. Both of them seemed uncomfortable. Something here disturbed them rather than offered them the sweetness of God's redemption of man. She looked at Daniel, and the thought came to her that exactly the same perceptions were in his mind.

Brendan Flaherty was talking to a young woman, and his mother was hovering nearby, making movements as if she would interrupt. A middle-aged woman intruded. Mrs Flaherty flashed back at her with something that was clearly sharp, from the expressions of all of them. The girl blushed. The woman who spoke took a step backwards, and Brendan himself was hurt and turned away, leaving his mother standing defensively, but with no one to shield.

Fergal O'Bannion said something to him, mockery in his face, and put his hand over Maggie's. She froze, distress clear in her eyes. She said something to Fergal and closed her other hand over his. Watching them, Emily was certain it was restraint, not affection.

Brendan said something lightly, his voice too soft for Emily to hear anything of it. Maggie smiled and lowered her eyes. Fergal altered the way he was standing so that somehow in the moving of weight he had become vaguely belligerent.

Brendan looked at Maggie, and Emily thought she saw a tenderness in his expression that brought a shiver of awareness to her of a hunger far deeper than friendship. Then she looked again, and there was nothing more than a pleasant courtesy, and she was not sure she had seen anything at all.

She turned to Daniel to see if he had noticed it, but he was watching Padraic Yorke.

'It seems to have caught them hard,' Daniel said to her quietly.

She did not understand.

'The ship,' he explained. 'Do you suppose they knew some of the men? Or their families, maybe?'

'I don't think we know who they were,' she answered. 'Not that it matters. Anyone's death is a loss just the same. You don't have to have known them to feel it.'

'There's a weight in the air,' he said slowly. 'As if a spark of lightning would set it afire. It's good people they are.' His voice was so soft she barely heard it. 'To grieve so much for those they never knew. I guess that there's a common humanity in the best of us, and there's nothing like death to draw the living together.' He bit his lip. 'But I still wish I could mourn my fellows by name.'

Emily said nothing. It was not the loss of the others from the ship that haunted the village, it was the murder of Connor Riordan, and the certainty that it was one of them who was responsible.

'Of course,' she said after a moment's hesitation. The dead from the ship were his only connection with who he was, all that he had been and had loved. Without them he might never know again that part of himself. All they had endured together, the laughter, the triumph and the pain, could be lost. 'I'm sorry,' she added with profound feeling.

He smiled suddenly, and it changed every aspect of his face. Suddenly she could see in him the boy he had been a few years ago.

'But I'm alive, and it's poor thanks to the Good Lord who saved me if I'm not grateful for that, don't you think?' Then without waiting for her answer he walked towards the nearest small huddle of people and introduced himself, telling how much he appreciated their hospitality, and the courage of the men who had spent all night in the gale to bring him in alive.

She watched as he went to every person or group, saying the same thing, searching their faces, listening to their words. It occurred to Emily that it was almost as if he were trying desperately to find some echo of familiarity among them, someone who knew seamen, knew disaster, and understood him.

As they were drifting away and only half a dozen were left, she stood on the rough pathway between the gravestones and was only yards from where Father Tyndale was saying goodbye to an old gentleman with white hair, like down on the weed heads. Father Tyndale's eyes seemed to look beyond the man's face to where Daniel was talking to Brendan Flaherty, and she saw in him horror, as if this were what had happened before, in the days leading up to Connor Riordan's death.

Emily and Daniel walked home slowly along the road. Daniel seemed tired and she knew from the way he kept adjusting Hugo's coat on his shoulders that his body still ached from the bruises. Perhaps he was lucky that the wreckage hurled about by the sea had not injured him more. He seemed lost in thought, as if the underlying pain of the village had added to his own.

It could not go on like this. Someone must find the truth of Connor Riordan's death. Whatever it was, it had to be better than the corroding doubt. Daniel's presence had made the fear sharper than before, as if he had unknowingly woken it from sleeping.

He spoke suddenly, startling her. 'You're not Catholic, are you.' It was a statement.

'No,' she said with surprise. 'Sorry. Was I so out of place?'

He grinned. He had beautiful teeth, very white and a little uneven. 'Not at all. It's good to see it through the eyes of a stranger once in a while. We take it all for granted too easily. Was your aunt a Catholic before she came here and married?'

'No.'

'That's what I thought. It's a big thing she did. She must have loved him very much. I'd lay money – if I had any – that Connemara is not like where she came from.'

'You'd win,' she conceded, smiling back at him.

'More than double, I expect,' he said ruefully. 'And your family wouldn't be pleased.'

'No. My father – he's dead now – he was very upset.'

He looked at her, and she had the uncomfortable feeling that he knew she was evading the truth, making her part in it look kinder than it had been.

'You're Church of the English,' he concluded.

'Yes.'

'It's a big thing, so I've heard, this difference between us.

I don't know enough about the Church of the English to understand that. Is it so very different, then?'

'It's a matter of loyalty,' she replied, repeating what her father had said. 'The first is to our country.'

'I see.' He looked puzzled.

'No you don't!' She was not managing to say what she meant. 'It's your loyalty to Rome that's the problem.'

'Rome, is it? I thought it was to God . . . or Ireland?'

He was laughing at her, but she found it impossible to resent. Put like that, it was absurd. The whole estrangement was foolish, not about loyalties at all. Obedience and conformity were closer to the truth of it.

'You've not visited her here before?' he observed.

It would be pointless to deny it. She was obviously a stranger.

'She's ill now.' That was obvious too. She had made it sound as if that were the only reason she had come, and would not have were Susannah well. But then that also was true. In fact she would not even have now if Jack had not coerced her. It was his opinion of her that had made the difference. She cared what he thought of her more than she had realised. But that was none of Daniel's business either.

'And you've come to look after her?' he said.

'No. I've come to be with her over Christmas.'

'It's a good time to forgive,' he said with a slight nod.

'I'm not forgiving her,' Emily snapped.

He winced.

'I'm not forgiving her because there's nothing to forgive,' she said angrily. 'She's a right to marry anyone she chooses.'

'But your father had someone else in mind for her? Someone from the Church of the English? Perhaps with money?' He looked at Emily's fine woollen cape with its neat fur collar, then at her polished leather boots, suffering a little on the rough road.

'No, he didn't. Our family is comfortable, not more than that. My first husband had money, and a title. He died.'

'I'm sorry.' His compassion was instant.

'Thank you. But I love my second husband very much.' She sounded defensive and she heard it in her own voice.

'Has he money and a title as well?' Daniel asked.

'No he hasn't!' She said it as if it had been faintly insulting to ask. 'He has neither, nor any prospects. I married him because I love him. He is a Member of Parliament and he does some very fine work.'

'And is your father very happy, then? Oh . . . I forgot. You said he was dead too. Did he mind you marrying a man with no title or prospects?' He was keeping exact step with her on the rough road. 'Did you dare his anger, like your aunt Susannah? I see now why you are here with her. You have a natural sympathy. Not exactly a black sheep of the family, but at least one of a different colour?'

She wanted to laugh, and be furious, and she was embarrassed because she had taken a wild risk in marrying Jack Radley. He had had no money at all, and she had had a great deal, but even more than that, he flirted outrageously, and made his way by being such an entertaining guest at other people's house parties that he hardly ever had to pay towards the roof over his head. But he was fun, he was kind, and when things were hard and dangerous, he was brave. The best qualities within himself he had discovered after they were married.

But she had accepted him without having to dare her father's wrath, or lose a penny of her own money inherited as a widow. Would she have had the courage to marry Jack even if it had not been so easy? She hoped so, but she had not had to prove it. Compared with Susannah she was shallow, and yet she had passed judgement so easily.

'It's very good of you to be here, over Christmas especially,' Daniel interrupted her thoughts. 'Your husband will miss you.'

'I hope so,' she said with an intensity of feeling that surprised her. Would Jack be missing her? He had been very quick to insist that she went. She tried to recall the last few weeks before that letter from Thomas had arrived. How close had she and Jack been, beyond the courtesy of habit? He was always agreeable. But then he was to everyone. And as she had just reminded herself, it was she who had the money. Or more correctly, it was her son Edward – George's son, not Jack's. Ashworth Hall, and all that went with it, was her inheritance only through him.

Was Jack missing her? Or might he perhaps be enjoying himself accepting the sympathy, and the hospitality, of half the women in London who found him nearly as attractive as Emily did?

She became unpleasantly aware that Daniel was watching her, studying her face as if he could read her emotions in it. She had given herself away with 'I hope so'.

'He will be looking after my children,' she said a little abruptly. Then she wished she had said 'our children'. 'Mine' sounded proprietorial, defensive. But to go back and correct it would make her sound even more vulnerable.

'Very good of you,' he repeated. 'Has Susannah children? She does not speak of them, and there are no pictures.'

'No, she doesn't.'

'So there is only you?'

'Not at all!' That sounded awful, as if she had abandoned Susannah all those years. 'My mother is travelling in Europe and my sister is unwell.'

'She is an invalid?'

'Not at all. She is very healthy indeed, she simply has a touch of bronchitis.'

'So she will miss the Christmas parties too.'

'She does not go to parties very much. She is married to a policeman – of high rank.' She did not know why she added that last bit. Pitt had been quite lowly when Charlotte had married him. She too had married for love, not caring much what anyone else thought. And looking back, Emily missed the days when she and Charlotte had played a part in some of Pitt's most difficult cases. Since he had been in Special

Branch, such help had been rarely possible. Balls, theatre, dinners were all fun, but lacking in depth after a while, a superficial world, full of wit and glamour, but no passion.

'I've hurt you,' Daniel said with contrition. 'I'm sorry. You have been so kind to me I wished to know you better. I think I asked insensitive questions. Please forgive me.'

'Not at all,' Emily lied, needing immediately to deny that he had struck any truths. She had no unhappiness, and he mustn't think she had. She looked at him to make sure he understood. He was smiling, but she could not read what lay behind his eyes. She was left thinking that he had understood her far better than she wished.

With a sudden and very painful clarity she remembered what Father Tyndale had said about Connor Riordan asking questions, exposing the vulnerable so it could no longer be lied about or ignored. Whose dreams had he stripped so unbearably? Had he even known he was doing it? Was it now happening again, beginning with her?

Should she pursue it? Dare she? The alternative might be worse: cowardice that would allow the village to die. She would have to bend her mind very seriously to detecting, not merely skirt around the edges, beginning fears and doubts, and completing nothing. She could awaken even uglier things than were stirring. Once begun, it would be morally impossible to stop before all the truth was laid bare. Was she ready for that? Was she even competent to do such a thing, let alone deal with the results?

She would very much rather not tell Susannah – she had more than enough distress to deal with – and yet Emily could not succeed without her help. She realised as she said that to herself that she had already made up her mind. Failure might be a tragedy, but not to attempt was defeat.

Emily did not get the opportunity to speak to Susannah alone until afternoon teatime when Daniel had gone back to sleep, still aching from his deep bruises and finding himself overcome by tiredness, and perhaps as much by grief. She had given little thought to the loneliness he must be feeling, the loss to which he could put no names or faces, only a consuming void.

Emily and Susannah sat by the fire with tea and scones, butter, jam and cream. Emily missed the bright flames of a coal or log fire, but she was growing used to the earthy smell of peat.

She told Susannah of the morning at church, and then of her walk back with Daniel, the questions he had asked and how his probing had disturbed her thoughts, making her realise what Father Tyndale had meant of Connor Riordan.

Susannah sat still for a long time without replying, her face bleak and troubled.

'Is that not what you wanted me here for really?' Emily asked gently, leaning forward a little. She disliked being quite so blunt, but she had no idea how long they had in which to pursue this.

'Actually I wrote to Charlotte,' Susannah said apologetically. 'But that was before Thomas told me that you actually helped him quite a lot as well, in the beginning. I'm sorry. That's ungracious, but we have no time left for polite evasions.'

'No,' Emily agreed. 'I need your help. Are you wishing to give it? If not, let us agree that we do nothing.'

Susannah winced. 'Do nothing. That sounds so . . . weak, so dishonest.'

'Or discreet?' Emily suggested.

'In this case that is a euphemism for cowardly,' Susannah told her.

'What are you afraid of? That it will have been someone you like?'

'Of course.'

'Isn't knowing it's one person better than suspecting everybody?'

Susannah was very pale, even in the glow of the candlelight. 'Unless it is someone I care for especially.'

'Like Father Tyndale?'

'It couldn't be him,' Susannah said instantly.

'Or someone Hugo cared for?' Emily added. 'Or protected?'

Susannah smiled. 'You think I am afraid it was him, to protect the village from Connor's probing eyes.'

'Aren't you?' Emily hated saying it, but once the question was asked, evasion was as powerful as an answer.

'You didn't know Hugo,' Susannah said softly, and her voice was filled with tenderness. It was as if the years since his death vanished away and he had only just gone out of the door for a walk, not for ever. 'It's not my fear you are speaking about, my dear, it is your own.'

Emily was incredulous. 'My own? It doesn't matter to me who killed Connor Riordan, except as it affects you.'

'Not your fear of that,' Susannah corrected. 'Your doubts about Jack, wondering if he loves you, if he's missing you as much as you hope. Perhaps a little realisation that you don't know him as well as he knows you.'

Emily was stunned. Those thoughts had barely even risen to a conscious level of her mind, and yet here was Susannah speaking them aloud, and the denial that rose to her lips would be pointless. 'What makes you think that?' she said huskily.

Susannah's expression was very gentle. 'The way you speak of him. You love him, but there is so much of which you know nothing. He is a young man, barely forty, and yet you have not met his parents, and if he has brothers and sisters, you say nothing of them, and it seems, neither does he. You share what he does now, in Parliament and in society, but what do you know or share of who he was before you met, and what has made him who he is?'

Suddenly Emily had the feeling that she was on the edge of a precipice, and losing her balance. This was the night of the Duchess's dinner. Was Jack there? Who was he sitting beside? Did he miss her?

Susannah touched her softly, just with the tips of her fingers. 'It is probably of little importance. It does not mean it is anything ugly, but the fact that you do not know suggests that it frightens you. I don't believe it is that you don't care. If you love him, all that he is matters to you.'

'He never speaks of it,' Emily said quietly. 'So I do not ask. I made my family serve for both of us.' She looked up at Susannah. 'You love Hugo's people, don't you? This village, this wild country, the shore, even the sea.'

'Yes,' Susannah answered. 'At first I found it hard, and strange, but I became used to it, and then as its beauty wove itself into my life, I began to love it. Now I wouldn't like to live anywhere else. And not just because Hugo lived and died here, but for itself. The people have been good to me. They have allowed me to become one of them and belong. I don't want to leave them with this unresolved, whatever the answer is. I don't want to go with it unfinished.'

'Then help me, and I will do anything I can to find the answer,' Emily promised.

Emily started to think about it seriously that evening, but she was too tired after so much missed sleep with the storm, and it was the following morning before she felt her mind was clear enough to be sensible.

She went for a brisk walk, this time not towards the village but in the opposite direction, along the shore and around where the rock pools were, and the wind rustling in the grass.

After seven years the questions of means and opportunity to kill Connor Riordan would be difficult, or even impossible to answer. The only clues would lie in motive. Whose secrets could Connor Riordan have known that were dangerous enough, and painful enough for him to be killed? Had he known anyone in the village before he was washed up that night?

When Maggie O'Bannion came to clear out the fires, and do some of the other heavy jobs, such as the bed linen, Emily decided to help her, partly because she felt uncomfortable doing nothing, but actually more to give her the chance to speak naturally with Maggie as they worked together.

'Oh, no, Mrs Radley, I can do it myself for sure,' Maggie protested at first, but when Emily insisted she was happy enough. Emily did not tell her how long it was since she had done any housework of her own, although Maggie might have guessed from her clumsiness to begin with.

'Daniel seems to be recovering,' Emily remarked as they put the towels into the big copper boiler in the laundry room, and added the soap. 'Although it's taking time.'

'Course it is, poor boy,' Maggie agreed, smiling when she saw Emily's surprise that it was bought soap, not home-made.

Emily blushed. 'I can remember making it,' she said, although Maggie had made no remark.

'Mr Ross always did things very nicely,' Maggie replied. 'Went to Galway once a fortnight at least, and got the best things for her, right up until he died.'

'He wasn't ill?' Emily asked.

'No. All of a sudden, it was. Heart attack, out there on the hillside. Died where he'd have wanted to. And a better man you'll never meet.'

'His family is from around here?' Now Emily was sweeping the floor with the broom, a job she could hardly mishandle. Maggie was busy mixing ingredients to make more furniture polish. It smelled of lavender, and something else, sharper and extremely pleasant.

'Oh, yes,' Maggie said enthusiastically. 'A cousin of Humanity Dick Martin, he was.'

'Humanity Dick?' Emily was amused, but had no idea who she was talking about. A local hero, presumably.

'King of Connemara, they called him,' Maggie said with a smile, her shoulders a little straighter. 'Spent his whole life saving animals from cruelty. Over in London, most of the time.'

'Are they worse to animals in London than here?' Emily tried to keep the offence out of her voice.

'Not at all. He was a Member of Parliament, and that's where they change the laws.'

'Oh, yes, of course.' She made a mental note to ask Jack if he had heard of Humanity Dick. But now she must bring the conversation back to the thing she needed to know. 'Daniel still hasn't any memory yet.' She felt as if she were being ungraciously obvious, but she could think of no subtler way of approaching it. 'Do you suppose the ship was making for Galway? Where would it have come from?'

'You're thinking we should see what we can do to help him,' Maggie said thoughtfully. 'Thing is, it could have been anywhere: Sligo, Donegal, or even further than that.'

'Does his accent tell you nothing?' Emily asked. 'I don't know in Ireland, but at home I might have an idea. I would at least know Lancashire from Northumberland.'

'And would that help you, then?' Maggie said with interest. 'I heard England was a very big place, with millions of people.'

Emily sighed. 'Yes, of course you're right. It wouldn't help much. But Ireland has far fewer, hasn't it?' That was only a polite question. She knew the answer.

'Yes, but it's different being a seaman. They pick up expressions from all over the place, and accents too, sometimes. I'm not good at it. I can hear he's not from this bit of coast, but it doesn't even have to be north that he's from, does it? It could be anywhere. Cork, or Killarny, or even Dublin.'

Emily bent and brushed up the dirt into a dustpan, not that there was much. It was a gesture rather than a real task. 'No, you are right. He could be from anywhere. Were most of the people in the village born here?'

'Just about all. Mr Yorke comes from Galway, I think, but I dare say his family are from one of the villages closer. His roots are deep. If you want to know the history, he's the man to ask. It's not just the tales he can tell you, but the meanings behind them.' She smiled a little ruefully. 'All the old feuds between the Flahertys and the Conneeleys, the good works of the Rosses and the Martins – and the bad too – and the love stories and the fights going back to the days of the Kings of Ireland in the time before history.'

'Really? Then I must see if he will tell me.' Emily accepted the idea, although it was not the ancient past she was seeking. Again she tried to bring the conversation back to the present. 'The Flahertys seem interesting. What was Seamus Flaherty like? I gather Brendan takes after him a lot?'

Maggie avoided her eyes and started to watch what she was doing with great care. 'Oh, I suppose so,' she said casually, but there was a tension in her voice. 'In a superficial sort of way. He certainly looks like him. Same eyes, same way of walking, as if he owned the world, but was happy for you to have a share in it.'

Emily smiled. 'Did you like him?' she asked.

Maggie was silent, her back stiff, her hands moving more slowly.

'Seamus, I mean,' Emily clarified.

'Oh, well enough, I suppose,' Maggie started to move briskly again. 'As long as you didn't take him too seriously, he was fine enough.'

'Seriously?'

'Well, you couldn't trust him,' Maggie elaborated. 'Charm the birds out of the sky, he could, and make you laugh till you couldn't get your breath. But half of what he said was nonsense. Got the moon in his eyes, that one. And drank most men under the table.'

'An eye for the women?' Emily asked bluntly.

Maggie blushed. 'Oh, for sure. That was one thing you could rely on. That, and a fist fight.'

Emily did not need to ask if Mrs Flaherty had loved him; she had seen it in her face. Behind the over-protection of her son, the slight distance she placed between herself and others, there was a deep vulnerability. Now its explanation was easy to see.

But Emily also heard in Maggie's voice a tenderness, a self-consciousness that betrayed her too, not for the father, but for the son. Was that also a defence of one of their own, a man too easily misunderstood by an English stranger? Or was it more than that?

She bent her attention to helping complete the household tasks. Maggie did the ironing, quite a skilled work when the two flat irons had to be heated alternately on the stove, and used at a narrow range of temperatures, not so hot so it scorched the linen, nor too cool to press out the creases.

Emily peeled and sliced vegetables and set them in cold water until Maggie was ready to make the stew.

In the afternoon Emily walked along the shore to the shop. They needed more tea, sugar and a few other things. The air was fresh and crisp, but with no sting of ice in it, as there would have been in London. It was still westerly off the ocean, and the salt and kelp were in every breath. The sky was clouded far out to sea, but overhead it was clear blue with only a few thunderclouds towering in bright drifts, moving slowly, dazzling white.

The shore itself was uneven, sand obliterating some of the old grass and flower-strewn stretches, dunes moved from one place to another as if she had mistaken where they had been. Here and there were tangles of weed, some kelp torn up from the deep beds and left dark and untidy on the sand. She could not help seeing the jagged ends of wood poking out of them, splinters of the ship that had gone down, as if the sea could not digest it but had cast it back. It was a kind of monument to human daring, and grief.

It was when she stopped to stare at one of the larger pieces, pale, raw ends of wood jutting up through the black tangle of weed, that she became aware of Padraic Yorke standing a little behind her. She turned and looked into his eyes, and saw a reflection of the same overwhelming sadness that she felt, and of the fear that the power and beauty of the sea gives rise to when one lives through all its moods.

'Do you get wrecks like this every winter?' she asked.

'Not only winter,' he replied. 'But the storms are very rarely as bad as this one was.' His face looked pinched, hollow around the eyes, and she wondered if he too was thinking of that other storm, seven years ago, and the young man who had been washed up then, and had never left.

'Daniel still can't remember anything,' she said impulsively. 'Do you think anyone here could help?'

'How?' He was puzzled. 'No one knows him, if that's what

you mean? He isn't related to anyone in the village, or any of the other villages around.' He smiled bleakly. 'Everyone is related to everyone else, or knows who is. It's a wild country. Its people belong. They have to. He isn't from anywhere in the west of Connemara, Mrs Radley.'

It seemed a preposterous thing to say, an assumption he could not have reason to make. And yet she believed him. 'You know the land well enough to say that?'

His face lit. 'Yes, I do. I know the land, and all the people who live here, and their history.' He gazed around him, narrowing his eyes a little as he looked across the high tussock grasses where the wind knifed through them, tugging, swaying and rippling all the way to the hills against the horizon. The colours changed, moving with every shadow. One moment paler, the next undershot with darkness, then a faint patina of gold.

Perhaps he saw some momentary wonder in her face, or possibly he had been going to speak anyway. 'Before you leave, you must go to the bog,' he told her. 'At first it'll seem desolate to you, but the longer you look, the more you will see that every yard of it shows you some flower, some leaf, a beauty that'll haunt you always after that.'

She smiled in spite of herself. 'I'd like to. Thank you. But tell me about the people. I can't understand the land without knowing some of the people it shaped.'

They had left the splintered wood and tangles of weed, but she was happy to walk slowly. She had all afternoon, and she wanted to learn what he had to say.

'Is Brendan Flaherty really so wild?' she said with a slight smile. 'Of course I only saw the charming side of him, when he and his mother visited Susannah.'

Mr Yorke gave a shrug, lifting one shoulder more than the other, making the gesture oddly humorous. 'He used to be, but there's no harm in him. He pushed the rules to the limit, and beyond, when he was younger. No scrape in the village he wasn't involved in, one way or another. And no pretty girl he didn't flirt with. How far any of that went I don't know, and I didn't ask. I suppose he was over the edge, at times. But that's what happens when you're young.'

'But not real trouble?' Emily found herself defensive, remembering sharply the flash of hurt she had seen in Brendan's eyes.

'Of course not,' Mr Yorke said ruefully. 'His mother would always see to that. She spoiled him from the beginning. And after his father died, nothing was too good for him.'

'How do you mean?' She needed to understand, not to assume. Could Connor have challenged Brendan in some way, and having always been given anything he wanted, Brendan could not bear losing? Had there been a fight, a flare of temper, blows, and suddenly Connor was dead? Mrs Flaherty would have covered for Brendan, excused him, lied for him, as she had always done. Perhaps believing it was an accident, Hugo Ross would have too.

Was it necessary? Or did they fear that Brendan was going to show that element beyond indiscipline, the true selfishness that destroys? Was it fear that Emily had seen in Colleen Flaherty's face when she watched her son, or only an anxiety that others would believe of him what they had witnessed in his father?

Was it true? And had Connor Riordan come into the village, with vision not clouded by history and excuses, and seen Brendan more clearly than others? Or was Mrs Flaherty's fear only her own experience with the husband she was so in love with, crowding out the truth that Brendan was another man, a different one. She could not cling on to her husband, or put right what may have been wrong, revisit the old failings.

Was that what Emily had seen in Brendan's eyes? A fear that he was turning into his father, with his father's weaknesses? Or a fear that his mother would neither see him for himself, or allow him to be free of Seamus's ghost, and still love him?

Was she still protecting him because he needed it, or because *she* did? Did she feed his weaknesses so he would still need her, rather than curbing them?

Had Connor seen that, and probed the wound? Sometimes legends matter more than reality, dreams more than truth. Would Daniel see it too?

'Thank you, Mr Yorke,' Emily said suddenly. 'You are right. I may very well come to see a beauty in the bog that I had not thought possible.'

She went on quickly now, aware that she was cold. She

was glad to reach the shop and go inside where it was agreeably warm.

'Good day to you, Mrs Radley,' Mary O'Donnell said with a smile. 'A bit chill it is, for sure. Now what can I get for you? I have some nice heather honey, which I saved for poor Mrs Ross. Very fond of it, she is. And it'll do her good.' She bent down and picked a jar from below the counter. 'And a dozen fresh eggs,' she went on. 'What with that poor creature washed up by the sea, an' all, you'll be cooking more than usual. How is he, then?'

'Bruised,' Emily replied. 'I think he was a bit more seriously injured than he said at first. But he'll recover.'

'And stopping here in the meantime, no doubt.' Mary pulled her lips tight.

'Where would he go?' Emily asked.

'Some mother's missing him,' Mary responded. 'God comfort the poor creature.'

Emily put the shopping into her basket and paid for it. 'The shop is quiet this afternoon,' she observed, allowing a slight look of concern into her expression.

Mary's gaze moved away, as if caught by something else, except there was nothing, no movement except the wind.

'It'll get busy later, I dare say,' she said with a smile.

Emily knew she would learn nothing if she did not ask. 'I met Mr Yorke along the beach. He was telling me something of the history of the village.'

'Oh, he would,' Mary agreed, relieved to have something

general to talk about. 'Knows more than anyone about the place.'

'And the people,' Emily added.

The light vanished from Mary's eyes. 'That too, I suppose. By the way, Mrs Radley, I have half a loaf of bread here for Mrs Flaherty. If you're going that way, would you mind dropping it in for her?' She produced a bag, carefully wrapped. It was not quite an invitation to conclude the conversation, but the suggestion was there.

Emily seized it. 'Of course. I would be happy to.'

Immediately Mary gave her directions to the Flaherty house.

'You can't miss it,' she said warmly. 'It's the only one along that road with stone gateposts and two trees in the front. And would you mind taking a pound of butter at the same time?'

Mrs Flaherty looked startled to see Emily on the doorstep.

Emily held out the loaf and the butter, explaining how she came to have them.

Mrs Flaherty took them, and without seeming deliberately discourteous, since Emily remained standing on the doorstep, she invited her in to have a cup of tea. Emily accepted immediately.

The kitchen was warm from the big stove against the wall, and the polished copper pans gave it a comfortable feeling, along with strings of onions hanging from the ceiling beams, the bunches of herbs and the blue and white china on the old wooden dresser.

'What a lovely room,' Emily said spontaneously.

'Thank you,' Mrs Flaherty smiled. She pushed the kettle over on to the hob and started taking down cups and saucers. She had gone to the larder to fetch milk when a movement outside the window caught Emily's eye. She was staring into the garden, watching Brendan Flaherty deep in conversation with someone just beyond her sight when Mrs Flaherty returned. She glanced outside and saw Brendan, and her face filled with a kind of exasperated pride as she looked at him. He was holding up a carved wooden frame, such as might have fitted around a painting.

'His father made that,' Mrs Flaherty said quietly. 'Seamus had wonderful hands, and he loved the wood. Knew the grain of it, which way it wanted to go, as if it spoke to him.'

'Has Brendan the same gift?' Emily asked, watching as Brendan's hand caressed the piece he held.

A shadow crossed Mrs Flaherty's face. 'Oh, he's like his father inasmuch as one man can be like another.' Her voice was low and hollow with a kind of regret, and in that moment Emily had a sudden awareness of Mrs Flaherty's loneliness, and how different it was from Susannah's. It was incomplete, there were doubts in it, things unresolved.

Then Brendan moved and Emily saw that it was Daniel he was talking to. Daniel laughed and held out his hand. Brendan gave him the wooden frame. Daniel's eyes met his, and he said something. Brendan put his hand on Daniel's shoulder.

Mrs Flaherty dropped the cups and saucers the short

distance on to the table with a clatter and strode to the back kitchen door. She threw it open and went outside.

Brendan turned, startled. His hand dropped from Daniel's shoulder. He looked embarrassed. Daniel simply stared at Mrs Flaherty as if she were incomprehensible.

She snatched the carved frame out of his hands. 'That isn't Brendan's to give,' she said hoarsely. 'None of his father's work is. I don't know what you want here, young man, but you aren't getting it.'

'Mother—' Brendan began.

She turned on him. 'You don't give away your father's work until you can equal it!' she told him fiercely, her voice shaking.

'Mother—' Brendan began again.

Daniel cut across him. 'He wasn't giving me anything, Mrs Flaherty. He only showed it to me. He's proud of his father, as you would want him to be.'

Mrs Flaherty's cheeks were flaming now. She was confused, wrong footed without knowing how it had happened, and still angry.

'Perhaps I had better walk Daniel home, and not trouble you just now,' Emily interrupted. 'I'll accept your invitation for tea another time.' She could see the hot embarrassment in Brendan's face as he glared at his mother, and the next moment looked away, searching for words without finding them.

'Thank you,' Daniel accepted, looking at Emily, then taking a step towards her. He swivelled slightly and smiled at

Brendan, with gentleness and a quick flash of amusement in it. Then touching Emily lightly on the arm, he guided her along the path to the gate, and the road.

As Emily latched the gate behind them, she saw Brendan and Mrs Flaherty arguing fiercely. Once Mrs Flaherty jabbed her finger towards the road, without looking or seeing Emily staring at her. Brendan was shouting back, but she could not hear the words, only his shaking head made it clear he was denying something.

Daniel was looking at her. 'Poor Brendan,' he said sadly. 'Competing with the ghosts?'

'Ghosts?' she asked as they began to walk back along the road towards the shore. 'His father. Who else?'

'I don't know,' he replied with a quick smile. 'Whoever it was that he liked, and his mother is so afraid of.'

He was right. It had been fear she had seen in Mrs Flaherty's eyes. Why? Was it an unsuitable friendship? Was she jealous, afraid of losing some part of him – his time, his attention, his need? Might someone else take from her the role of his protector?

Or was she afraid of something that Brendan might do? Did it concern Connor Riordan's death? Was that why the sight of his friendship with Daniel had woken such fear in her? History repeating itself?

Later in the afternoon Emily made the opportunity to speak to Susannah alone, and tried to find the words to ask her.

'Daniel seems to have made something of a friendship

with Brendan Flaherty,' she remarked casually. They were standing in the drawing room looking out of the long window at the storm-battered garden.

'Oh, really?' Susannah said with some surprise.

Emily seized on it. 'Mrs Flaherty was very upset. She disapproved so violently she practically ordered Daniel to leave, and it embarrassed Brendan acutely.'

Susannah looked confused. 'Are you sure?'

'Yes. Does that have anything to do with Connor Riordan?'

'How could it?'

'Were they friends too?'

'Are you asking me if Brendan killed him?' Susannah said in surprise. 'I have no idea. I can't think why he would.'

Emily refused to give up. 'We don't know why anyone would, but it is inescapable that somebody did. Why is Mrs Flaherty so protective of Brendan? You know them. Was his father really so wild, and is Brendan the same? He seems very likeable to me, and more gentle than Mrs Flaherty.'

Susannah smiled. 'Seamus Flaherty was a drinker, a brawler and a womaniser. Mrs Flaherty is afraid Brendan will be the same. He looks like his father, but I don't know that it's much more than that.'

'He isn't married, though,' Emily pointed out. 'Does he have girls in the different villages? Or one after another?'

Susannah was amused. 'Not more than most young men, so far as I know. But if he did, that might get him killed, but not Connor Riordan.'

Emily abandoned the pursuit, and went for a walk in the fading sun, watching it die over the sea in the long winter twilight. She heard the crunch of footsteps on the gravel and Daniel came up the shore towards her. The wind had stung some colour into his cheeks and his dark hair was tangled. He climbed up the slithering shingle to where she stood, and waited beside her for several moments before speaking. The fading light sharpened his features, making the hollow of his cheeks more pronounced, the lines of his mouth and the lean curve of his throat. He was almost beautiful.

Emily was achieving nothing. She had tried subtlety and observation. Time was closing in. Perhaps in a few days Daniel would go, or even worse, Susannah's health would fail and Emily would not learn what had happened to Connor Riordan in time. The village remained steeped in its poison.

'Did Brendan Flaherty make a sexual advance towards you?' she said impulsively, and was shocked at her own directness.

Daniel's mouth dropped open and he stared at her in amazement. Then he started to laugh. It was a joyous sound, bubbling up inside him in total spontaneity.

Emily felt her face burning, but she refused to look away. 'Did he?' she insisted.

Daniel controlled himself and the laughter died away. 'No, he most certainly didn't. He's more patient with his mother than many a man might be, but there's nothing of that sort about him.'

'I wasn't thinking of his mother,' Emily said tartly. 'She's terrified he's going to be a womaniser like his father, and a drunkard. And yet she admired him. She wants Brendan to be just like him, and yet she doesn't. There's no way he could succeed for her.'

'Ah! So wrong, and yet so right,' Daniel said appreciatively. 'Ask Mrs O'Bannion. Though I doubt she'll tell you. Come on, let's go back to the house. You'll catch your death standing here. That wind off the sea has knife blades in it.' He offered her his hand to balance as she stepped down over the rough shingle into the sand.

When they got home Susannah was in the kitchen. She looked pale – drained of all strength.

'What is it?' Emily said quickly, going towards her and putting her arm around her to support her weight.

'I'm all right,' Susannah said impatiently, although it was obviously not true. 'I was just putting things out ready for breakfast.'

'Maggie'll do that in the morning,' Emily told her.

'No,' Susannah said with a little catch in her voice. 'Fergal came by to say she won't be coming any more. I'm sorry. It will mean more work for you, until I can find someone else.'

Emily was appalled, but she tried to mask it. 'Don't worry,' she said with all the strength of conviction she could assume. 'We'll manage very well. I used to know something about cooking. I'm sure I can manage again. We'll be fine. Now please go to bed.'

Susannah gave her a weak smile, barely touching the corner of her lips, and together they made a slow and painful way up the stairs.

Emily woke in the night with a sense of unease. The wind was rising again and she thought she could hear something banging. She got up, wrapping her shawl around her and tiptoed out onto the landing. She could still hear the rattle, but now it seemed to be more the wind in the chimneys, and even if there were a slate loose, there was nothing she could do about it.

As she was turning she saw the light under Susannah's door. She hesitated a moment, wondering whether to intrude or not, then there was a flicker of movement, shadows across the light, and she knew Susannah was up. She went to the door and knocked. There was no answer. The tension tightened inside her, fear for Susannah overwhelming her. She turned the handle and went in.

Susannah was standing by the bed, her face completely colourless, her hair straggling and damp. There were dark shadows around her eyes as if she were bruised, and her nightgown clung damply to her skeletal body.

Emily did not need to ask if she were feverish, or even if she had been sick. The bed linen was tangled, trailing on the floor to one side, and Susannah was shaking.

Emily took off her shawl and wrapped it around Susannah's shoulders, then guided her to the bedroom chair. 'Sit here for a few minutes,' she said gently. 'I'll go and put my clothes on, then I'll heat some water, get clean towels, and remake the bed. I know where the linen cupboard is. Just wait for me.'

Susannah nodded, too spent to argue.

Emily had very little idea what she was doing, except to try to make Susannah as comfortable as she could. She had no experience in nursing the sick. Even her own children had always had a nanny for the occasional colds or stomach upsets. Susannah was dying, Emily knew she could do nothing to prevent it, and she realised how intensely that mattered to her. Care no longer had anything to do with duty, or even with earning Jack's good opinion.

When she was dressed she went downstairs, lighting the candles on the way, and banked up the fire to heat the water. If she were as ill as Susannah, she imagined she would long to be in a clean and uncrumpled bed, and perhaps not alone. Not spoken to, but just to know that if she opened her eyes, someone would be there.

It did not take her more than half an hour to strip the bed and remake it with clean linen, but in doing so she noticed that there was only one more set of sheets. She would have to launder tomorrow, without Maggie.

When the bed was ready, she carried up a bowl of warm water, and helped Susannah to strip off her soiled nightgown. She was horrified at how gaunt her body was, her flesh sunken until her skin seemed to hang empty on her arms and across her stomach. The mercy of clothes had hidden it before, and

Susannah was not so ill as to be unaware of the change in herself.

Emily struggled to hide her fear at the wasting of disease, the change from a beautiful woman to one who was a ghost of her old self. She washed her gently, patting her dry because she was afraid the rub of the towel would bruise her, or even tear the fragile skin.

Afterwards she helped her into a clean nightgown, and half carried her to the bed.

'Thank you,' Susannah said with a faint smile. 'I'll be all right now.' She lay back on the pillows, too exhausted to attempt concealing it.

'Of course you will,' Emily agreed, and sat in the armchair near the bed. 'But I have no intention of leaving you.'

Susannah closed her eyes, and seemed to drift into a light sleep.

Emily stayed there all night. Susannah stirred several times, and at about four in the morning, when the wind was higher, for some time she felt as if she might be sick again, but eventually the nausea passed away and she lay back. Emily went down to the kitchen and made her a cup of weak tea, and brought it up, offering it to her only after it had considerably cooled.

By daylight Emily was stiff and her eyes ached with tiredness, but there had been no more episodes, and Susannah seemed to be asleep and breathing without difficulty.

Emily went down to the kitchen to make herself tea and

toast to see if she could revive her strength enough to begin the laundry.

She was halfway through the tasks when Daniel came in. 'You look bad,' he said with sufficient sympathy to rob the words of insult. 'Did the wind keep you up?'

'No. Susannah was ill. I'm afraid you're going to have to get your own breakfast, and maybe luncheon as well. With Maggie not coming I've too much to do to be cooking for you.'

'I'll help you,' he said quickly. 'Toast will be fine. Maybe I'll fry an egg or two. Can I do one for you as well?'

'No, I'll do the eggs. You fetch the peat in and stoke the fires,' Emily replied. 'I've got sheets to wash, and in this weather it won't be easy to get them dry.'

He looked up. 'There's an airing rail,' he pointed out. 'We'd best keep the kitchen warm and use that. Rough dry will have to do, if that's all we have time for.'

'Thank you,' she accepted.

'Is she bad?' he asked.

'Yes.' She had not the will or the strength to keep it from him.

'Maggie shouldn't have gone,' he shook his head. 'That's my fault.'

'Is it? Why?' She asked not because she doubted him, but she needed the reason explained.

He looked a little uncomfortable. 'Because I upset her. I was asking questions.'

'About what?'

'People,' he replied. 'The village. She told me about Connor Riordan, some years ago. It was a powerful memory for her.'

'Was it?' Emily ignored the kettle, merely pushing it to the side off the hob. 'Why? Did she know him well?'

His dark eyes were puzzled. 'What are you trying to do, Mrs Radley? Find out who killed him? Why do you want to know, after all this time?'

'Because his death is eating the heart out of the village,' she replied. 'It was someone here who killed him, and everybody knows that.'

'Did Susannah ask you to? Is that why you came? You haven't come before, have you, in all the years she's been here? And yet I think you care for her.'

'I . . .' Emily began, intending to say that she had always cared for Susannah, but it was not true and the lie died on her tongue. Again she thought, is this how Connor Riordan was, seeing too much, saying too much? And with that thought the ice-like grip in the pit of her stomach tightened. Was it all going to happen again? Would Daniel also be murdered, and the village die a little more? She realised that not only was he right in that she cared for Susannah, she cared about him also.

'I'm sorry,' he apologised ruefully. 'You've been up all night trying to help Susannah, watching her suffer and knowing there's nothing you can do except be there, and wait, and I'm not helping. I'll get the peat in and see to the fires, and I'll start the laundry. That can't be too hard. But first we'll eat.'

She smiled back at him, the warmth opening inside her like a slow blossom. She would find out what happened to Connor Riordan, and she would make absolutely certain it did not happen again, however difficult that was, and whatever it cost her.

She and Daniel had just finished the heavy laundry when Father Tyndale arrived. They had the sheets put through the mangle until they were twisted as dry as possible, then she hung them on the airing rail in the kitchen, winched up to where the warm air from the stove would reach them. Father Tyndale looked tired in spite of the rosy colour in his face from the buffeting of the wind. He seemed almost bruised by it, and his eyes watered in the warmth of the room.

'I'll take you up to see Susannah,' Emily said, immensely relieved to see him. His mere presence lifted the responsibility from her. As long as he was here, she was not alone. 'She had a bad night, so don't be surprised to see her looking ill. I'll bring you both tea as soon as I make it.'

'Thank you.' He looked at her closely, and she knew he saw her own weariness, and perhaps something of the fear in her, however he made no remark on it, simply following her up the stairs.

'Father Tyndale?' Susannah said quickly, pulling herself up in the bed and lifting her hand to tidy her hair into some semblance of the beauty it had once had. Emily fetched the comb and did it for her. She even wondered whether to bring some of her own rouge to put a little colour in Susannah's white cheeks, but decided it would look artificial, and deceive no one. She finished the hair instead, smiling back in approval before turning to invite Father Tyndale to come in.

She went back downstairs. This was a conversation that should have complete privacy. She returned with tea and a little thinly sliced bread and butter, hoping that with company Susannah would be able to eat.

It was over an hour later when Father Tyndale came into the kitchen carrying the tray with him. Daniel was occupied with jobs outside, and Emily was busy with vegetables ready for lunch, and then dinner. Before she came here it had been years since she'd done such tasks herself.

Father Tyndale sat in one of the hard-backed chairs, looking tired and too big for it.

'Brendan Flaherty has left the village,' he said quietly. 'No one knows where he's gone, except maybe his mother, and she won't say.'

Emily was stunned. Her instant thought was that the quarrel between Brendan and his mother was much worse than she had assumed at the time. Then she wondered if it was whatever Daniel had said to him. What was Brendan running away from? The past, or the future? Or both?

'I was there at Mrs Flaherty's house yesterday,' she said hesitantly. 'Daniel was there, but out in the garden, talking to Brendan. Mrs Flaherty saw them and was very angry. She went out and told Daniel to leave, pretty abruptly.'

Father Tyndale looked troubled, searching for words he knew already that he would not find.

She wanted to tell him about her suspicion that Brendan might have had some relationship with Connor Riordan that Mrs Flaherty disapproved of violently, but she did not know how to frame it without offending him. 'She was very upset,' she said again. 'As if she were afraid of him.' She took a deep breath. 'Was it Connor she was seeing in her mind? Why else would she be so fierce with Daniel? He's only been here a couple of days.'

'She's afraid of many things,' he replied. 'Sometimes history repeats itself, especially if you fear that it will.'

'Was Brendan close to Connor?' She was being evasive, saying nothing much, but always at the forefront of her mind was this man's calling as a priest.

'You didn't know Connor,' he said softly. 'He was a stranger here, and yet he seemed to know everything about us. It might have been something of himself he was looking for, but it was disturbing none the less.' He smiled at her, and changed the subject to Susannah's illness, and all that they might do to make things easier for her.

When he had gone Emily was annoyed with herself for having been so ineffectual. She stood in the kitchen, staring out of the window. The wind was harsher, the sky grey and bleak. She was afraid Susannah would die soon, before anything was resolved. She hugged her shawl around herself, cold inside, amazed to realise how much it mattered to her. Daniel was right, she cared about Susannah, not for the aunt of her childhood with whom her father had been so angry, but for the woman now who loved the village that had welcomed her, and who were the people of the man with whom she had shared so much happiness.

Who could help heal the wound in them? She needed someone who was an observer, not personally involved with the loves and hates of the village. And as soon as she had framed the question to herself, she knew the answer. Padraic Yorke.

After making sure that Susannah was well enough to leave for a short time, Emily put on a heavy cloak and walked in the wind to Padraic Yorke's house. She knocked on the door and received no answer. She was cold and impatient. She needed his help, and yet she was unhappy away from the house for any longer than was necessary. She shivered and wrapped the cloak more closely around her. She knocked again, and again there was no answer.

She looked at the house, very neat, traditional. There was a tidy garden with herbs. Like everywhere else, most of them were cut back or had withdrawn into the earth for winter. This would gain her nothing. She was growing colder by the moment, and Mr Yorke was clearly not in.

She turned and walked down by the shore. She did not want to be in the open wind off the water, but the turbulence of the sea was like a living thing, and the vitality of it drew her, as she felt it might have drawn Padraic Yorke also.

She walked along the edge of the sand. The waves broke with a sustained roar, varying in pitch only slightly. Beyond the last dark mound of kelp she saw the lone, slender figure of Padraic Yorke.

He did not look round until she was almost up to him, then he turned. He did not speak, as though the broken wood in the kelp, and the water spoke for themselves.

'Brendan Flaherty's gone from the village,' Emily said after a moment or two. 'Susannah is very ill. I don't think she's going to live a great deal longer.'

'I'm sorry,' he replied simply.

'Where would he go, and why now?' she asked.

Mr Yorke's face was bleak. 'Do you mean so close to Christmas?'

'No, I mean with Daniel here.' She told him of the scene that she and Mrs Flaherty had witnessed through the kitchen window.

'The Flahertys have a long history in the village,' he said thoughtfully. 'Seamus was one of the more colourful parts. Wild in his youth, didn't marry until he was over forty, and even then near broke Colleen's heart more than once. But she adored him, forgave him with more excuses than he could think of himself.'

'And for Brendan too?' she asked.

He shot a quick glance at her. 'Yes. And a poor gift it was to him.'

'Do you know where he will have gone, or why?'

'No.' He was silent for several moments. The waves continued pounding the shore and the gulls wheeled above, their cries snatched away by the wind. 'But I could guess,' he continued suddenly. 'Colleen Flaherty loved her husband, and she wants her son to be like him, and yet she also wants to keep a better control of him, so he can't hurt her the way Seamus did.'

Èmily had a sudden vision of a frightened and lonely woman deluding herself she had a second chance to capture something she had missed in the beginning. No wonder Brendan was angry, and yet unwilling to retaliate. Why had he finally broken away?

'Thank you for telling me,' she said with profound gratitude, and a sense of humility. 'You have helped me to realise why Susannah loves the people here. It is remarkable that they accepted her so well. None of you has much cause to make the English welcome.' She felt a sense of shame as she said it, and that was an entirely new experience for her. All her life she had thought of being English as a blessing, like being clever or beautiful, a grace that should be honoured, but never questioned.

Mr Yorke smiled, but there was embarrassment in his eyes. 'Yes,' he said quietly. 'They are good people; quick to fight, long to hold a grudge, but brave to a fault, never beaten by misfortune, and generous. They have a faith in life.'

Emily thanked him again and started walking back towards

the path to Susannah's house. As she reached the road she saw Father Tyndale in the distance walking the other way, his head bowed as he turned into the wind, struggling against it. She doubted he would agree with Mr Yorke that the people of the village had a faith in life. The murder of Connor Riordan had set a slow poison in them, and they were dying. She must find the truth, even if it destroyed one of them, or more, because not knowing was killing them all.

Susannah had another bad night and Emily sat up with her through nearly all of it. The hour or so of sleep she snatched was spent still propped upright in the big chair near the bed. She ached to help, but there was little she could do except sit with her, occasionally hold her in her arms, when she was drenched with sweat, wash and dry her, help her into a clean nightgown. Several times she brought her warm tea, to try to keep some fluid in her body.

Daniel came in quietly and stoked the fire. He took the soiled and crumpled sheets and nightgown away, saying nothing, but his face was pale and racked with pity.

A little before dawn Susannah was sleeping at last, and Daniel said he would watch with her. Emily was too grateful to argue. She crept to her bed and when at last she was warm, she slept.

It was broad daylight when she woke and after a moment's bewilderment she remembered how ill Susannah had been, and that she had left Daniel alone to look after her. She threw the covers back, scrambled out of bed and dressed hastily. First she went along the corridor to Susannah's room. She found her sleeping quietly, almost peacefully, and Daniel in the chair looking pale, hollows around his eyes, the dark shadow of stubble on his chin.

He looked up at her and held his finger to his lips in a gesture of silence, then he smiled.

'I'll go and get breakfast,' she whispered. 'Then we'll do the laundry. I can't do it without your help. I've no idea how to get that wretched boiler working.'

'I'll be there,' he promised.

But when Emily went down the stairs she found the lamps all lit in the kitchen and a smell of baking filling the air. Maggie O'Bannion was at the sink washing dishes after her making and rolling of pastry.

She turned at the sound of Emily's step. 'How's Mrs Ross?' she asked anxiously.

Emily was too relieved to see her to show her anger. 'Very ill,' she said truthfully. 'That was the second really bad night. I'm very glad indeed that Mr O'Bannion relented. We don't know how to manage without you.'

Maggie blinked and looked away. 'I've made an apple pie for dinner,' she said as if Emily had asked. 'And there's a good piece of beef in the oven. I'll save some of it to make beef tea for Mrs Ross. Sometimes if she's ill she can hold that but not much else. Is she awake, do you know?'

'No, she's not. She didn't get much sleep last night.' Emily saw that Maggie felt guilty, and she was glad of it. 'I'll get to the washing,' she went on. 'Daniel helped me yesterday, but there are more sheets this morning.' She glanced up at the crumpled linen on the airing rack close to the ceiling. 'We aren't as efficient as you are,' she added more gently.

Maggie said nothing, but her hands moved more quickly in the sink, and she banged the dishes together roughly.

Emily put the flat irons on the hob to heat, then wound the airing rack down and took two of the sheets off it. Automatically Maggie turned from the sink to help her fold them neatly. She did not meet Emily's eyes and there was a tension in her shoulders of a deep unhappiness.

Emily wondered if Daniel had left yesterday afternoon, perhaps when Father Tyndale was here, and gone to tell Maggie how much she was missed. And was Maggie's tension this morning caused because she and Fergal had quarrelled about it? What had Daniel said to her that she had defied her husband?

When the sheets were folded ready to iron, Emily began on the pillowcases, then stopped briefly for a cup of tea and a slice of toast. She was wondering if she should go up to see if Susannah was awake when Daniel came into the kitchen.

'Good morning, Mrs O'Bannion,' he said cheerfully. 'I'm more grateful to see you back than you can imagine. We weren't managing so well without you.'

Maggie shot him a sharp glance, and neither of them looked at Emily.

'Susannah's awake,' Daniel went on. 'Can I take some breakfast up to her, if there's something like bread and butter, or at least a fresh cup of tea?'

'You have something yourself,' Emily told him. 'I'll take it up to Susannah, and you can do something with those sheets. We'll need them again soon enough. Maggie, if you could speak softly to the boiler and get it going again, we need to do last night's sheets for when we need them. Please?'

'Yes, Mrs Radley, of course,' Maggie agreed a trifle stiffly, and, avoiding Daniel, she began to cut thin bread and butter for Susannah, carefully spreading the softened butter on the cut end of the loaf, and then slicing it so razor-thin it barely held together. Then she buttered and halved a second slice and a third, arranging them daintily on a blue and white plate.

Emily thanked her and took the tray. She was extraordinarily pleased when Susannah sat up, a faint touch of colour in her cheeks, and ate all of it. Emily decided she must remember how it was done and make it herself another time.

An hour later Susannah was dozing and Emily went downstairs again to catch up on some of the household chores she was behind with, and which took her so much longer than it had Maggie.

She stopped at the kitchen door when she heard voices, and then laughter, a man and a woman. It was a rich sound, a welling-up of a kind of happiness.

'Really?' Maggie said with disbelief.

'I swear,' Daniel replied. 'Trouble is, I can't remember how long ago it was, or why I was there.'

'It sounds marvellous,' Maggie said wistfully. 'I sometimes dream about going to places like that, but I don't suppose I ever will.'

'You could, if you wanted to,' Daniel assured her.

Emily stood motionless, not making a sound. She could see Maggie's face as she looked at Daniel. She was smiling, but there was a wistfulness in her eyes that betrayed her dreams, and that she believed them beyond her reach.

'Not everything you want can be had for the asking,' she said to him. 'It's wise to know what to grasp for, and what will only hurt you.'

'It's not wise,' Daniel replied gently. 'It's owning defeat before you've even tried. How do you know what you can reach, if you don't stretch out?'

'You talk like a dreamer,' she said sadly. 'One with his feet way off the ground, and no responsibilities.'

'Is that what it is that holds your feet hard to the earth, then? Or is it Fergal's feet you mean?' he questioned in return.

Maggie hesitated.

In the doorway Emily froze. Had Daniel been telling her stories of travel and adventure, disturbing her contentment with hunger that could never be fed?

'Maybe you could go to Europe?' Daniel suggested. 'Find a charm that would feed your heart for ever afterwards. There are magic places, Maggie. Places where wonderful things happened, great battles, ideas to set the world alight, love stories to break your heart, and then mend it again all in a new shape. There's music, and laughter till you can hardly breathe from the ache of it! There's food you couldn't imagine, and tales to carry with you to fill the winter nights for every year to come. Wouldn't you like that?'

Emily came in quickly, intending to interrupt them, then she saw Maggie's face and changed her mind. There was a vulnerability in it that was startling, but she was not looking at Daniel, rather into some thoughts of her own.

Emily was suddenly chilled. She remembered how gentle Daniel had been with her when they were walking back from church, how soft his questions were, how natural. And yet they had dug more deeply than she wished, exposing weaknesses she had not acknowledged to herself. Now he was doing the same thing to Maggie, uncovering the loneliness in her, the disappointment. Emily had seen Fergal O'Bannion, a good man but without wings of the mind. He was possessive of her. Was that because he had seen her laugh with Connor Riordan, listen to him, join in his tales and his dreams? And now she was listening to Daniel, and so Fergal had commanded Maggie not to be in this house, and she had disobeyed him? To help Susannah, or to listen to Daniel?

Emily recalled odd remarks, very slight, only glancing, but were they the ugly tips of fact? Had Maggie escaped the enclosing bounds of her life for a brief passion with Connor, and Fergal knew it? Was that why Connor had been killed? The oldest of reasons?

Did Maggie know that? Or at least fear it?

And yet Mrs Flaherty feared it was Brendan who had killed Connor, and Brendan had disappeared.

'Wouldn't you like to, Maggie?' Daniel repeated, his voice gentle.

Emily stepped forward and saw him. He was smiling and as he folded the sheet over, his slender hand lingered for a moment over Maggie's.

Emily felt the heat burn up inside her and drew in her breath to speak.

'I have things to fill my winter nights, and dreams in plenty already,' Maggie replied. 'There's nothing I want you to add to them, Daniel. I like your tales of places you've been, and I hope by telling them perhaps you've recalled a thing or two of who you are. That's all. Do you understand me?'

'Yes, I understand you,' he said quietly. 'Perhaps I expected too much help in my own fancies. A dose of reality can do wonders.' He smiled at his own error, gently self-mocking, and Emily saw Maggie ease a little, smiling back. The moment of embarrassment passed.

Daniel moved away, and as he left the kitchen he brushed by Emily, and realised that she must have overheard the conversation. He could not know how long she had been there, but at the very least she had seen Maggie rebuff him. He pulled a slightly rueful face as he caught her eye, and she was at that moment absolutely certain that he knew exactly what she was trying to do to solve the murder of Connor Riordan, and why she was driven to try. Even so, it made no difference. Emily went on into the kitchen as if she had merely passed him in the passage.

'How is she?' Maggie asked, a faint flush on her cheeks all that there was left from her conversation with Daniel.

'Definitely improving,' Emily said cheerfully. 'I'm sure she is less anxious now that you are back. I'm grateful to you for returning.' She tried to soften her voice to rob the words of offence, but she had no hesitation in speaking them. 'Did Daniel come to you yesterday and tell you how ill Susannah was?'

'Yes,' Maggie answered. 'I'm so sorry. If I'd known, I wouldn't have stayed away even for a day.'

There was such unhappiness in her face Emily did not doubt her. 'It's difficult to know how much to obey one's husband, against the voice of one's own conscience,' Emily responded with more honesty than she had expected. What would she do to please Jack, against her own judgement? How often had he asked her? She realised that the journey to Connemara was probably the first time. Except that it was not against her conscience so much as in response to his. It should have been she who wanted to come, and he who tried to dissuade her.

But what if she had wanted to come, and he had been against it, what would she have done? Made obedience an excuse? Or love? She did love Jack, she hated quarrelling with him. But they quarrelled very seldom. Why was that? Could it be a lack of passion, or even of conviction? What did she care about enough to do, even if it cost her something? And if there were nothing, what did that say of her? Something too terrible to own.

'Fergal is not a harsh man, Mrs Radley,' Maggie was saying, stopping her work to try to explain. It mattered to her that Emily did not judge him coldly. 'He didn't know Mrs Ross was so bad, and he took Daniel wrong. It all goes back to the other wreck. I dare say you don't know much about that. Fergal got a wrong idea in his head, and it could be I was to blame for it.'

Emily could not turn away from such a perfect chance. 'You mean Daniel reminds Fergal of Connor Riordan, and he thought history was playing itself out all over again?' she asked.

Maggie lowered her eyes. 'Well, something like that.'

Emily deliberately sat down at the kitchen table. 'What was Connor like, really? Please be honest with me, Maggie. Is history repeating itself in Daniel?'

Maggie put the linen down and bit her own lip as she weighed her answer. 'Connor was funny and wise, like Daniel,' she answered. 'He made us all laugh. We liked his tales of where he'd been, strange lands he'd visited . . .'

'Like Daniel just now?' Emily interrupted.

'Yes, I suppose so. And like Daniel, he was interested in

everyone. He kept on asking questions, and we answered because it seemed only kindness that made him say such things. You know how it is when you talk to someone, and they like you, want to know about you, what you like, what your dreams are? You get to thinking. It's rare enough someone wants to know about you instead of all about themselves.'

Emily admitted ruefully that that was true.

'Connor was interested in everyone,' Maggie went on. 'I liked him. He was different. He told us new stories, not the same old ones. He made me think, look at everything a bit differently. But I wasn't the only one to feel at times as if he could look into my mind too easily, and too deep. There are things sometimes best not known.'

'Things about love, and jealousy, and debts?' Emily asked.

Maggie's voice dropped. 'I suppose so. And dreams that shouldn't be told.'

'We'd die without dreams,' Emily replied. 'But you're right, some of them shouldn't be told to others.'

'I love Fergal,' Maggie said quickly, and on that instant Emily knew that it was at least in part a lie.

'But Connor had a fire of the mind,' Emily finished for her. 'And Fergal was a bore by comparison, and he came to know it.' She was afraid now that she was too close to the truth, and that if she tore off the last covering it would destroy Maggie's world.

'Fergal is a good man,' Maggie repeated stubbornly, as if saying it could make it true. 'Sure, I liked Connor's tales, but that's all. I didn't love him. You're wrong in that, Mrs Radley. Like, that's all, because he made me think, and made me laugh. He taught us all how to see a wider world than this village and its loves and hates.'

'But he saw your loneliness, and he made Fergal see it too.' Emily could not let it go. The pictures were all becoming clearer.

Maggie blinked away tears. 'It can hurt very deep to have to face a truth you've been hiding from. It's my fault too. I told Fergal what he wanted to hear, and then felt cheated when he believed me and looked no further. I suppose I let him think I was in love with Connor, and he with me. God forgive me for that.'

So Maggie had allowed Fergal to think she was in love with Connor. Was she afraid that it was actually Fergal who had killed him, and inadvertently she had been responsible for it? And now she would protect him, because of her own guilt?

Had she loved someone else? If not Connor, then who?

How much of any of it had Susannah seen, or guessed? And was she telling the truth when she had claimed to be so certain Hugo Ross had known nothing of the passions and weaknesses of these people whose lives for good and ill were so woven with his own?

Father Tyndale came to see Susannah again in the afternoon, and stayed for over an hour. Emily walked most of the way home with him. The wind was gusty, and cold with the chill of the sea, and in spite of its violence she found the salt and the smell of the weed had a kind of bitter cleanness that pleased her.

'I think she hasn't long now,' Father Tyndale said gravely, forcing his voice to carry above the wind.

'I know,' Emily agreed. 'I hope it isn't before Christmas.' Then she did not know why she had said that. It was not Christmas that was the issue, it was learning the truth about Connor Riordan, and whatever it proved to be, letting Susannah believe there was some resolution in it, a healing for the people she loved.

'Tell me more about Hugo, Father,' she asked.

He smiled as they walked down through the rough grass, still mounded with the debris of the storm, then into a clear stretch of the beach. It was a longer way to his house, but to take it felt right to both of them.

'How hard it is to say anything that gives any idea of what they were really like,' Father Tyndale answered thoughtfully. 'He was a big man, not just physically, with a big man's gentleness, but he was broad of spirit. He loved this land and its people. But then his family have been here as long as even the legends tell. He made his money in business, but his pleasure was painting, and he might have been good enough to keep himself that way, if he'd tried. Heaven knows, Susannah never asked for wealth. She was happy just to be with him.'

'And his faith?' she enquired.

'You know,' he said with slight surprise, 'I never asked him. I took it for granted from the way he was that he knew there was a greater power than all of mankind, and that it was a good power. Some people talk a lot about what they believe, and the laws they keep, the prayers they say. Hugo never did. He came to church most Sundays, but whatever guilts or griefs he had, he sorted them with God himself.'

'Is that all right with you?' she questioned.

'He loved his fellow men, without judgement,' he answered. 'And he loved the earth in all its seasons. To me, that meant he loved God. Yes, that's all right with me.'

'You didn't mind him marrying an Englishwoman?' she said, almost joking, not quite.

He laughed. 'Yes, I did. Not that it made a ha'penny's difference. His family weren't happy either. They'd have liked him to find a nice young Catholic girl, and have lots of children. But he loved Susannah, and he never asked anyone else what they thought.'

'But she became Catholic,' Emily pointed out.

'Oh, yes, but not because he ever asked her to. She did it for his sake, and in time she came to believe.'

She changed the subject. 'What did Hugo think of Connor Riordan?' She had to ask, but she realised she was afraid of the answer. Surely the man Father Tyndale had known would have seen the damage Connor was doing, the secrets he seemed to understand too easily, the fears and hungers he awoke?

They were walking along the shore, around the wreckage. Father Tyndale did not answer her.

'Where has Brendan Flaherty gone, Father?' she asked. 'And why? Was his father alive when Connor was killed?'

'Seamus? No, he was dead by then. But even the dead have secrets. Some of his were uglier than Colleen guessed at.'

'But Brendan knows?'

'Yes. And Hugo knew. I think that was why he tried to take Connor back to Galway, but that winter the weather was bad. We had hard and heavy rain, with an edge of sleet on it. And Connor was too frail to go all that way. Five hours in an open cart would have all but killed him. He wasn't as strong as Daniel. Swallowed more of the sea, I think, and half drowned in it for longer too. It's a hard thing to come close to death. I'm not sure that his lungs ever got over it.'

'Did he come from Galway?'

'Connor? I don't know if it was where he was born, or simply where his ship put out from. He spoke like a Galway man.'

'And Hugo wanted to take him back there?'

'Yes. But he knew he couldn't, not until he was stronger, and the weather turned.'

'Then it was too late?'

'Yes.' His face crumpled in grief. 'God forgive us.'

They were the first ones to walk along the sand since the ebb. There were no footsteps ahead of them, just the bare, hard stretch between the waves and the tide line.

'Was Hugo afraid even then that something would happen, Father?'

He did not answer.

'Were you?' she insisted.

'God knows, I should have been,' he said heavily. 'These are my people. I've known many of them all their lives. I hear their confessions, I speak to them every day, I see their loves and their quarrels, their illnesses, their hopes and their disappointments. How could all this have happened, and I did not see it? God forgive me, I still don't.' He continued a few paces in silence, then went on as if he had forgotten she was there. 'I can't even help them now. They are frightened, one of them is carrying a burden of guilt that is eating his soul, and yet none of them comes to me for intercession with God, for a chance to lay down the weight that is crushing the life out of them, and find absolution. Why not? How have I failed so completely?'

Emily had no answer. Everyone had shame for something, at some time in their lives. What could it have been that Connor Riordan had seen, or guessed? Did it threaten one of the people here whose frailty he knew, and could protect? Even Susannah?

She did not want to hear. She wished she had never embarked on detecting. She was not equipped to succeed, or to deal with the inevitable tragedies that it would bring. She should have had the courage, and the humility, to tell Susannah that in the beginning. What arrogance of hers to imagine she could come in here, a stranger, and solve the grief of seven years!

She looked at Father Tyndale's bent shoulders and his sad face, and wished she could give him some comfort, some hand to grasp in the faith that should have buoyed him up. He believed he had failed his people, his lack of trust in God, or understanding His ways had caused their failure too.

She had nothing to say that would help.

It was late afternoon, close to dusk, when Emily made her decision. She would need help not only from Father Tyndale, but from Maggie O'Bannion, and possibly from Fergal as well. There was no point in telling Susannah until she was sure the plan would work. She would much rather have waited until her aunt was a little better, but that might not happen. The weather could close in and make it impossible.

Or worse than any of that, whoever had killed Connor might see in Daniel the past occurring again, and kill him too.

She walked through the darkening evening, bright only in the west over the sea, which heaved grey like metal, scarlet from the sun pouring over it as if it were spilled blood. She knocked on Maggie's door.

Maggie answered, and when she saw Emily the blood drained from her face.

'No,' Emily said quickly. 'She's not worse. In fact I think she's quite a bit better. I want to take the chance to go to

Galway. I'll have to be there two nights, at the least. Will you stay in the house with Susannah, please? I can't leave her alone. At night she's too ill. And I can't expect Daniel to care for her. Anyway, she should have a woman, someone she knows, and trusts. Please?'

Fergal had come to the door behind her. His face was dark with memory, and guilt. 'No,' he said before Maggie could speak. 'Whatever you want to go to Galway for, Mrs Radley, it'll have to wait. And you can't expect Father Tyndale to leave the village now either. Poor Mrs Ross could pass any day. Isn't that what you came for? To be with her?' There was challenge in the line of his jaw and the hard brilliance of his eyes.

'I'm not going for myself, Mr O'Bannion,' Emily said, trying to keep the anger out of her voice. 'It is for Susannah—'

'She has all she needs here,' he cut her off.

'No, she doesn't. She—'

'Maggie's not staying in that house with Daniel, and that's an end of it,' he told her. 'Good night, Mrs Radley.'

Maggie was still standing in the doorway and although he reached for the door to close it, she did not move. 'Why are you going to Galway?' she asked Emily. 'Is it to find out something about Connor Riordan?'

'Yes. Hugo Ross went, and I need to know why.' Emily had not wanted to say that, but now it was forced out of her. 'And maybe someone there will know Daniel.' She turned to Fergal. 'If Daniel stays with Father Tyndale until I come back, and you go to Susannah's as well, will you allow Maggie to stay there then?'

'Yes, he will,' Maggie said before Fergal could answer.

'Maggie—' he protested.

'Yes, you will,' she repeated, glancing at him only briefly. 'It is the right thing to do, and we all know that.'

He sighed, and Emily saw him look at Maggie with a tenderness that transformed his face, and a loneliness that would have torn her heart if she had seen it.

'You'd best go tomorrow,' he told Emily. 'The weather's going to get worse again in a day or two. It won't be a storm like the big one, but it'll be too bad for you to drive a pony across the moors, even Father Tyndale's Jenny. We'll come tomorrow morning. You'll be wanting to set out by nine.'

'Thank you,' she said warmly. 'I'm grateful.'

Then she went to Father Tyndale again and told him her plan, asking to borrow Jenny and trap, and if Daniel could stay with him until she returned. He agreed with her, warned her of the weather, told her he could not leave the village when Susannah was so ill.

'I know,' she said immediately. 'But what is the alternative? To say to her that I've given up?'

He sighed. 'I'll find one of the men from the village to go with you. Rob Molloy, perhaps, or Michael Flanagan.'

'No . . . thank you,' she said quickly. 'Someone from this village killed Connor. I'm safer alone, and if no one knows that I've gone. Please?'

Father Tyndale's mouth pulled tight and his eyes were black and hurt, but he did not argue. He promised to have the pony and trap ready for her at nine in the morning. She said she would prefer to walk to his house than have him collect her.

She followed the road back to Susannah's. It was now completely dark and she was glad of the lantern she had brought. The wind was hard and heavy, and colder.

She set out in the morning after having gone briefly to say goodbye to Susannah. She had explained everything the previous evening, both where she was going and why, and that Daniel would be staying with Father Tyndale until she returned. She needed to give no reasons for that.

'I'll come back as soon as I can,' she said, watching Susannah's face to see in it the hope or the fear that she might not put into words. 'Are you sure you want me to go?' she added impulsively. 'I can change my mind, if you wish?'

Susannah looked pale, her face even more haggard, but there was no indecision in her. She smiled. 'Please go. I'm not afraid of dying, only of leaving this unsolved. The village has been good to me, they've allowed me to belong as if I were really one of them. They're Hugo's people, and I loved him more than I can ever explain. I'm quite ready to die, and to go wherever he is. That is really the only place I want to be. But I want to leave them something for all the love they've given me, but even more for the way he loved them. I want to see them begin to heal. Go, Emily, and whatever you find, bring it back. See that it is known, whether I'm here or not. And never feel guilty. You've given me the greatest gift you had, and I'm grateful to you.'

Emily leaned forward and kissed her white cheek, then walked out of the room, tears running swift and easy down her face.

It was a long and bitterly cold journey, but Jenny seemed to know it even without Emily's guidance, or Father Tyndale's instructions. The landscape had a desolate beauty, which now in a strange way comforted her. Even in the occasional drifting rain there was a depth that changed with the light, as if there were layer beneath layer in the grass. The stones shone bright where a shaft of sun caught them, and the mountains and the distance were full of shifting, ever-changing shadows.

When at last she reached Galway, with a little enquiry she found a hotel with stabling for the pony, and after a good meal and a change into dry clothes and boots, she set out to retrace Hugo's steps of seven years ago.

During the long drive she had given much thought to where Hugo would have begun looking for Connor's family. Father Tyndale had said Hugo possessed a quiet but deep faith, and that he went to church most Sundays. Surely he would begin by asking the churches in Galway if they knew of Connor Riordan's family? Whether they attended or not, the local priest would at least know of them?

It was easy to find a church; any passer-by could direct

her. It took a little longer to reach the one where the Riordan family was known, and it was after dark when she finally sat in the parlour of the rectory opposite Father Malahide and looked at his thin, gentle face in the candlelight. The room was filled with the earthy odour of peat, and the richness of tobacco smoke.

'How can I help you, Mrs Radley?' he said curiously. He did not ask what an Englishwoman was doing in Galway, having driven alone, in the middle of winter, all the way from the coast.

Briefly Emily told him about the storm and Daniel being the only survivor from the wreck. As her story progressed she saw in his face that he knew about Connor, with both pity and grief.

'Now Mrs Ross is very ill indeed,' she went on. 'I think she will not live much longer. There are things I need to resolve before then. Daniel's arrival has stirred old ghosts that need to be laid to rest, whatever the truth may be.'

'I cannot tell you what Hugo Ross said to me, Mrs Radley,' Father Malahide told her gently. 'He came to see if he could find Connor's family. The young man was too weak to come himself and all his shipmates were dead. Like your present young man, he seemed to be alone in the world, and to remember very little. I'm afraid many men are lost off the coast of Ireland, especially Connemara. The winter is very bad, and the weather sweeps in off the Atlantic with nothing to break it.'

'Did Hugo find any family for him?'

'Yes. His mother lived here in Galway. She worked in a foundling home run by the Church. She cared for the children who had no one else. She was not a nun, of course, but she had been there most of her adult life. I'm afraid there is nothing else I can tell you, Mrs Radley. All else was in confidence. I'm sure you understand that. I'm sorry to say it, but Connor's mother is dead now. Not that I imagine she could have helped you.'

'No,' Emily agreed gravely. 'I don't know if I will learn the truth of what happened to him, and it would be of little comfort to her to know. But someone else at the foundling home may be able to tell me what Hugo Ross was asking and perhaps what he was told.'

'Of course.' Father Malahide gave her the address and how to find the place, counselling her to go in the middle of the morning, when they would be best able to spare time to speak with her.

She thanked him, and walked as briskly as she could through the dark streets back to the inn where she was lodging.

In the morning she followed Father Malahide's directions and had no difficulty in finding the foundling home. It was a large, grey stone building with many additional outhouses, looking as if they had been adapted to be further accommodation.

Emily walked up to the front door and lifted the knocker. It was several minutes before it was answered by a slender little girl with a freckled face. Emily told her what she wished, and she was admitted to wait in a small, rather chilly anteroom with carefully stitched samplers on the wall, warning the would-be sinner that God sees all. Opposite it was a very large crucifix with a Christ-like figure in agony. It made Emily self-conscious and uncomfortable. She felt suddenly alien, and wondered at her wisdom in having come here at all.

She was conducted to see the matron in charge, a tired woman with a pale face, deeply lined, and the most beautiful brown hair in thick coils on her head.

Emily sat in her office and heard the busy tap of feet up and down the corridor and voices calling out cheerfully, hurrying people along, bidding a child be good, be quick, tie up her bootlaces, tuck his shirt in, stop chattering.

'I came to Connemara to stay with my aunt, Susannah Ross, who is very ill and will not live much longer,' she began frankly. 'Seven years ago her husband, Hugo Ross, came here looking for Mrs Riordan, because her son, Connor, was the only survivor of a shipwreck just off the coast where Mr Ross lived.'

'I remember him,' the matron said, nodding her head. 'He never returned, nor did the young man he spoke of. I'm afraid Mrs Riordan is dead now, God rest her soul.'

'Yes, I know. So is Mr Ross. And I'm afraid Connor was killed too,' Emily replied.

'Oh dear.' The matron's face showed genuine grief. 'I'm so sorry. Perhaps it's as well his poor mother never knew. She was so happy when Mr Ross told her Connor was saved from the wreck. So many men are drowned. The sea's a hard mistress, but you make a living where you can. The land can be hard too. So what is it I can do to help Mrs Ross now, poor creature?'

Emily had turned over and over in her mind what she would ask, and she was still uncertain, but now there was no more time for debate. She looked at this woman's tired eyes and the gnarled hands on her lap in front of her. She must have seen more than her share of grief. What kind of woman leaves her child to a foundling home to raise? Emily thought of her own children at home, and suddenly she missed them so intensely it was as if they had been torn from her. She could smell their skin, hear their voices, see the bright trust in their eyes. There was only one answer, a desperate woman, driven beyond the end of her strength, a hunted woman or a dying one.

'Connor Riordan was murdered,' she said bluntly and saw the matron wince as if she were familiar with that pain as well. 'We never found out who killed him, but I believe I know why. I have a deep fear that the same thing is going to happen again, this time to Daniel, if we do not prevent it. I think Hugo Ross may have learned something here that later told him who was responsible, and because he loved his people, he chose not to repeat it. He died shortly after Connor's death himself. He did not know that the poison of that guilt and fear was going to cause the village itself to die slowly. But his widow knows, and she wants above all things, before she dies, to put that right, perhaps for the village, but more, I think, for Hugo himself.'

'A good woman.' The matron nodded her head and made the sign of the cross with profound solemnity. 'I cannot tell you much myself, but I recall that he spoke for some time to Mrs Riordan, and that he asked quite a bit about Mrs Yorke. That seemed to distress him. I asked him if I could do anything to help him, and he said not. Mrs Riordan seemed upset as well, but when I spoke to her, she seemed to know little, but would not tell me why.'

'Mrs Yorke?' Emily said confused.

'Well, we called her Mrs,' the matron answered with a slight gesture of her hand, as if dismissing something trivial. 'But she was not actually married. She worked here for many years, then she too died. But it was her time. She was old, and ready to continue her journey towards God.'

'Old?' Emily was surprised. Was she Padraic Yorke's sister? Then she had to be considerably older than he. Or perhaps she was no relative. It was not a common name, but not unique by any means. 'Might she be a relation of Mr Padriac Yorke, who lives in the same village as Mrs Ross?'

'Yes, yes,' the matron said with a sigh. 'That she was. Though it's a long time now, poor soul.'

'A long time? But you said she was old!'

'So she was, not so far from eighty when she died. Must be fifteen years ago now, or maybe more.'

Suddenly Emily was far colder than the room explained.

Ugly thoughts crowded her mind, still shapeless. 'She wasn't his sister then?'

'No, my dear, she was his mother,' the matron said in surprise. 'She came here before he was born. At first she said she was a widow, with child, but later she was honest with us. She was never married. A respectable girl to begin with, in service to a family in Holyhead, in England. When the master of the house got her with child she took ship and came to Ireland. She started in Dublin, but when the child began to show she was thrown out, and came west to Galway, where we took her in. She was happy here, and stayed with us for the rest of her days. A good woman she was, and we gave her the courtesy of a married title.'

'So Padraic was born here?' Emily said incredulously. It was not that the shame of his early life appalled her, although it must have been hard enough, it was that in the eyes of the Irish he was an Englishman, by blood and breeding, if never at heart.

The matron nodded. 'Of course he had to leave when he was fourteen, because we couldn't keep him any longer. There are no funds for children once they are old enough to work, and there was nothing here for him. He was a good student. He went to Dublin for a while, then up to Sligo, and at last to the coast, where he stayed.'

'And Mrs Riordan knew all this,' Emily said slowly as the ugliness inside her head took its shape. Connor must have pieced it together, understanding exactly who Padraic Yorke was, not the Irish poet and patriot he said, but the illegitimate son of some rich Englishman and his cast-off maidservant. Would Connor have told anyone? Who dared take the chance that he would not?

'Thank you,' Emily said to the matron, standing up with sudden stiffness as if all her bones ached. 'I shall go back tomorrow to tell Susannah what I have learned. Then at least she will know. What she chooses to do about it is up to her.'

She spent the rest of the day in Galway because she did not dare take the long road back when she would make the last of the journey in the dark. She paid her bill after breakfast, and was on the road by nine, but it was with a heaviness inside her. She understood so easily why Hugo Ross had chosen to say nothing.

Padraic Yorke had killed Connor and it was probably murder. At the very best it was a fight that had gone disastrously wrong. But no one other than Yorke himself knew what had happened, the mockery, the laughter, the humiliation he might have suffered. It could have been a lashing out at unbearable jeering, perhaps even an obscene insult to his mother, surely a victim enough already. It could have been at least half an accident, never meant to end in death.

Or it could have been quite clearly a murder, even a blow from behind delivered the coward's way against a man who had come by information by chance, and had never intended to use it.

Had Hugo Ross known? Had he spoken to Padraic Yorke?

Or had he kept silence as well? Did he even know what he was concealing? She thought, from what Susannah had said of him, that probably he had known very well.

What he had not known was how the fear and the guilt would slowly poison the very fabric of the village until it was withering, day by day, a new suspicion here, a fear awakened there, another lie to cover an older one; Father Tyndale's self-doubt, and ultimately his doubt even of God.

She was past the lake and heading towards Oughterard, the wind tearing blue holes in a ragged sky and the sun brilliant on the hills. The slopes were almost gold, black stone ruins gleaming wet and sharp, when she saw a man in the road ahead of her. He was walking steadily, as if he were pacing himself to go far. She wondered if he lived in Oughterard. There was no house or farm anywhere in sight to either side of the road.

Should she offer him a lift? It seemed unwise. And yet it was inhumane to pass him and let him make his own way, against the wind on this rough road.

It was not until she was level with him that she recognised Brendan Flaherty. She pulled up the pony.

'Can I offer you a ride, Mr Flaherty?' she said. 'I'm heading home.'

'Home, is it?' he said with a smile. 'Sure, that's very good of you, Mrs Radley. And I'll be happy to drive for you, if you like. Though Jenny knows her way as well as I do.'

She accepted because she was tired, and although she was

a good rider, she was completely inexperienced at driving, and she was sure Jenny was aware of it.

They had gone well over a mile before Brendan spoke.

'I shouldn't have run away,' he said quietly, facing forward, avoiding her eyes.

'You're coming back,' she replied. Now that she knew the truth about Padraic Yorke she no longer had any fear of Brendan.

He gave a little grunt, wordless, but heavy with emotion.

She felt the weight of sadness in him, as if he were returning to an imprisonment.

'Why are you coming back?' she asked impulsively. 'Are you afraid that if you stay in Galway that you'll end up like your father, drinking too much, fighting, and in the end alone?'

'I'm not my father,' he said, keeping his eyes on the road.

She looked at him and saw that it was not anger but apology in his face, as if he had failed, and somchow hc had betrayed the expectations of his heritage.

'What was he like?' she asked. 'Honestly. Not your mother's dreams, but in truth. How did you see him?'

'I loved him,' he replied, seeking the words onc by onc. 'But I hated him too. He got away with being lazy, and cruel because he could make people laugh. He could sing like an angel. At least that's how I remember it. He had one of those soft voices full of music that makes every note sound easy. And he told stories about Connemara, the land and the people, so real that listening to him seemed as if the past ran like wine in your blood, a little drunk maybe, but so alive. Actually I think now that most of them were Padraic's stories anyhow, but he never seemed to mind my father telling them.'

'Did he know Padraic well?' she asked. There was a faint overcast coming across the sky, filling it with haze so the sun was no longer bright on the hills and some of the colour faded from the grass. It was going to get colder. There was a veil of rain to the north east over the Maumturk Hills.

'I don't know. I don't think so. But it wouldn't have made a difference. He'd have told the stories anyway. I asked Padraic one day if he minded, and he said my father only made them richer, and that was a good thing, for all of us, for Ireland.'

'He loves Ireland, doesn't he.' It was an observation; she intended no question in it.

Brendan looked at her. 'You didn't come to Galway looking for me, did you? I thought at first you did. I thought you might have wondered if I killed Connor Riordan . . . over Maggie. I didn't.' He said it vehemently, as if it were still somehow open to question.

Emily realised that that was what his mother was afraid of. She knew the violence in Seamus, perhaps she had even been a victim of it at times, and she imagined it in Brendan too, as if even Seamus's faults, repeated, could somehow keep him alive for her. No wonder Brendan had fled to Galway, or anywhere, to be free of the imprisonment of her dreams.

'I know you didn't,' she answered him.

He swung around to face her. 'Do you? Do you know it, or are you afraid to let me think you suspect me, in case I hurt you?'

'I know you didn't,' she told him. 'Because I know who did, with a far better reason than you have.'

'Do you?' He searched her face, and must have seen some honesty in it, because he smiled, and his clenched hands on the reins eased.

'You should say goodbye to your mother properly, and then go back to Galway, or Sligo, or even Dublin. Anywhere you want to,' she said.

'What about the village?' he asked. 'We're deceived by our own dreams. Padraic has taken our myths and polished them until they look the way he thinks they should, and we've come to believe it's the truth.'

'And it isn't?' although she knew the answer.

He smiled. 'He makes it more glamorous than it was. He creates saints that never existed, and making ordinary men with faults that were ugly and selfish into heroes with flaws that you love as much as their virtues. Then we've looked at the delusion because no one dares break the reflection in the glass.'

'And Connor Riordan saw that?'

He looked at her, a flare of understanding in his eyes. 'Yes. Connor saw everything. He saw that I love Maggie, and that Fergal doesn't know how to laugh and cry, and win her. And that my mother can't let my father lie in his grave as who he really was. And Father Tyndale thinks God has abandoned him because he can't save us against our will. And other things. I dare say he knew Kathleen and Mary O'Donnell and little Bridie, and everyone else.'

He did not mention Padraic Yorke, and she did not either. They drove the rest of the way in companionable silence, or speaking of the land and its seasons, and the old tales of the Flahertys and the Conneelys.

Emily set Brendan down in the middle of the village, then took Jenny and the trap back to Father Tyndale. He did not ask her what she had learned, and she did not tell him. Daniel walked back home with her, carrying her bag. He looked at her curiously, but he did not ask. She thought perhaps that he already guessed.

She finally sat alone with Susannah in the evening, when Maggie and Fergal had left, and Daniel was in the study reading. Susannah had a little colour back in her face, and she seemed briefly recovered again, though the faraway look in her eyes was still there, as if she were preparing to leave. Soon it would be Christmas Eve, and she was longing for the gift that Emily had for her.

'Hugo did know the truth,' Emily said gently, placing her hands over Susannah's thin fingers on the coverlet. They were upstairs, where Daniel could not possibly overhear them. 'Possibly more than we ever will. He did not tell it because he did not realise that the village's own fear would poison it, eating away its heart. If he had understood, I believe he would have told Father Tyndale, and let him see justice done.'

Susannah smiled slowly and the tears filled her eyes. 'Did you tell Father?'

'No. I will tell you, and you can do as you think best, whatever you think Hugo would have done, were he here,' Emily replied.

Then she recounted what she had learned in Galway, and added a little of her certainty about Brendan Flaherty also.

'I was afraid it could have been Brendan,' Susannah admitted. 'Or Fergal. He thought Maggie was in love with Connor.'

'I think she was in love with Connor's ideas, his imagination,' Emily said.

Susannah smiled. 'I think we all were. And afraid of him. He could sing too, you know, even better than Seamus. Colleen Flaherty hated him for that. I think he knew what a bully Seamus was too.' She sighed. 'Poor Padraic. Could it have been a fight, or an accident?'

'I don't know. But even if it was, Padraic let the village be poisoned by it.'

'Yes . . . I know.' They sat in silence for several moments. 'Father Tyndale has been to see me every day. He'll come tomorrow, and I'll tell him. Hugo would have.' Her fingers curled over Emily's and tightened. 'Thank you.'

The next day when Father Tyndale came in the morning Emily left him with Susannah and she walked alone along the shore towards the place where Connor Riordan had died. The marker stone was higher up, beyond where the sea reached, but she wished to stand where he had been alive, and tell his spirit that the truth was known. It could hardly matter, except to the living. Even Hugo Ross would know without her telling him. It was simply a sense of completion.

The waves were strong, hissing up the sand, gouging it out, sucking back in again and burying it under with deceptive violence. She could see how easily a slip of the footing could be fatal. No one would walk close to the waves' edge. Only emotion powerful enough to destroy all attention would lead anyone to be so careless. Had it been a fight?

She looked up across the dune and the tussock grass and saw Mrs Flaherty striding towards her, head forward, arms swinging purposefully. Emily kept on walking. She did not want to speak to Colleen Flaherty now, especially if Brendan had told her he was going to leave the village, perhaps never live here again. It would be a relief for Fergal, in time even for Maggie.

She walked on towards the place where Connor Riordan had died. The sand was softer under her feet. The last wave hissed, white tongued, up to within a yard of her.

Colleen Flaherty was gaining on her. Emily felt a sudden flicker of fear. She glanced landward and saw that the dune edge was too steep to climb here. The only way back was to retrace her steps. She was at the end of the open sand. She could see the grave marker. This was where Connor had died. The sea that was creeping upward, this wave wetting her feet, was the same undertow that had pulled him in, burying, drowning, giving him back only when the life had been battered out of him, as if rectifying what the storm had left undone. Now she was frozen, shivering, wet up to her knees, the heavy skirts dragging her down into the hungry sand.

Colleen Flaherty stopped in front of her, her face gleeful with a bitter triumph. 'That's right, Englishwoman. This is where he died, the young man from the sea who came here intruding into our lives. I don't know who killed him, but it wasn't my son. You should have left it alone and kept your prying to yourself.' She took another step forward.

Emily moved back, and the next wave caught her, almost taking her balance. She teetered wildly, waving her arms, and felt the sand suck her down.

'Dangerous seas here,' Mrs Flaherty said. 'Lots of people drown in them. You shouldn't have told Brendan to go away. It isn't any of your business. This is his land and his heritage. This is where he belongs.'

Emily tried to pull her feet unstuck and go towards her. 'It's time you let him go,' she said angrily. 'You're suffocating him. That isn't love, it's possession. He isn't Seamus and he doesn't want to be.'

'You don't know what he wants!' Mrs Flaherty shouted, taking a huge step towards Emily.

Emily struggled desperately and another wave washed in

and raced up the sand, catching her well above the knees and sending her flying, drenched in ice-cold water, fighting for breath. This is how it must have been for Connor Riordan, like the shipwreck all over again.

She saw Colleen Flaherty looming over her, then felt arms pulling her, and she had barely the strength to fight. There was another wave, burying them both, robbing her of breath. Then suddenly she was free and Padraic Yorke was holding her up. Mrs Flaherty was yards away. Emily gasped in the air. She was so cold it seemed to numb her entire body.

Another wave came and Padraic Yorke pushed her forward, towards the shore. She took another step. There were more people there but she was too battered to know who they were. Her lungs ached unbearably. Someone reached for her. Another wave came, but this time it did not take her. She was faint, stumbling, and then she pitched forward into darkness.

She awoke in her own bed in Susannah's house, still fighting for breath, and deathly cold inside.

'It's all right,' Father Tyndale said gently. 'It's all over. You're safe.'

She blinked. 'Over?'

'Yes. Colleen will be ashamed for the rest of her life, I think. And Padraic Yorke has made his restitution, may he rest in peace.' He made the sign of the cross.

She stared at him, understanding filling her slowly. 'Is he alive?'

'No,' he said softly. 'He gave his life to save you. It was what he wanted to do.'

She felt the tears prickle in her eyes, but she did not argue.

'Thank you, Mrs Radley,' he said softly, touching her hand. 'You have ended a long grief for us. Perhaps in a way you have given us a second chance. This time we will not turn away a stranger who brings us truth about ourselves that we might prefer not to know.'

She shook her head. 'It wasn't I, Father, it was circumstances that brought Daniel to the village, and gave us all an opportunity to face ourselves, and do it better this time. For me also. Perhaps that is what Christmas is, another chance. But it won't work if you don't tell everyone who killed Connor Riordan, and why.'

His face pinched. 'Can't we allow Padraic to die with his secrets? The poor man has paid. It might have been an accident. Connor was not Daniel, you know. He had a cruel tongue, at times. It may have been the blind cruelty of youth, but it hurts. The words cut just as deep.'

'No, Father, if they don't know who killed him, they will not lay their own suspicions away, and realise that it was the lies that hurt. No one needs to know what secret Padraic Yorke had, but we need to know our own.'

'Perhaps so,' he said reluctantly. 'If I had been honest with myself maybe all these bitter years need not have been. I wanted to save pain, but I only added to it. It was Hugo's debt too. I must thank Susannah for paying it.'

When, on Christmas Eve, the church bells began at midnight, Emily and Susannah sat before the fire listening to the wind in the eaves. Daniel had decided to walk to the service, and they were alone in the house.

Susannah smiled. 'I'm glad I can hear them,' she said gently. 'I wasn't sure if I would. Tomorrow will be a good day. Thank you, Emily.'

Headline hopes you have enjoyed *A Christmas Grace*, and invites you to sample the beginning of *A Christmas Promise*, another novel by Anne Perry, also available from Headline.

The week before Christmas, the smell and taste of it was in the air, a kind of excitement, an urgency about everything. Geese and rabbits hung outside butchers' shops and there were little pieces of holly on some people's doors. Postmen were extra busy. The streets were just as grey, the wind as hard and cold, the rain turning to sleet, but it wouldn't have seemed right if the backdrop to Christmas had been different.

Gracie Phipps was on an errand for her gran to get tuppence worth of potatoes and cabbage to go with the leftovers of dripping and onion to make a bubble and squeak for supper. Spike and Finn would pretty well eat anything they could fit into their mouths, but they liked this especially. Better with a slice of sausage, of course, but there was no money for that now. Every penny was being saved for Christmas.

She walked a little faster into the wind, pulling her shawl tighter around her. She had the potatoes in a string bag, along with half a cabbage. She saw the girl standing by the candle makers, on the corner of Heneage Street and Brick Lane, her reddish fair hair blowing about and her arms hugged around her as if she were freezing. She looked to be about eight, five years younger than Gracie, and skinny as an eel. She must be lost. She didn't belong here, or on Chicksand Street – one over. Gracie had lived on these streets ever since she had come to London from the country when her mother died six years ago, in 1877. She knew everyone.

'Are yer lost?' she asked as she reached the child. 'This is 'Eneage Street. Where d'yer come from?'

The girl looked at her with wide grey eyes, blinking fiercely in an attempt to stop the tears brimming over onto her cheeks. 'Thrawl Street,' she answered. That was two streets over to the west and the other side of Brick Lane, out of the neighbourhood altogether.

'It's that way.' Gracie pointed.

'I know where it is,' the girl replied, not making any effort to move. 'Me uncle Alf's been killed, an' Charlie's gone. I gotta find 'im, 'cos 'e'll be cold an' 'ungry, an' maybe scared.' Her eyes brimmed over again and she wiped her sleeve across her face and sniffed. ''Ave yer seen a donkey as yer don't know? 'E's grey, with brown eyes, an' a sort of pale bit round the end of 'is nose.' She looked at Gracie with sudden intense hope. ''E's about this 'igh.' She indicated, reaching upward with a small dirty hand.

Gracie would have liked to help, but she had seen no

animals at all, except for the coalman's horse at the end of the street, and a couple of stray dogs. Even hansom cabs didn't often come into this part of the East End. Commercial Street, or the Whitechapel Road maybe, on their way to somewhere else.

She looked at the child's eager face and felt her heart sink. 'Wot's yer name?' she asked.

'Minnie Maude Mudway,' the child replied. 'But I ain't lost. I'm looking fer Charlie. 'E's the one wot's lost, an' summink might 'ave 'appened to 'im. I told yer, me uncle Alf's been killed. Yesterday it were, an' Charlie's gone. 'E'd 'ave come 'ome if 'e could.'

Gracie was exasperated. The whole story made no sense. Why would Minnie Maude be worrying about a donkey that had wandered off, if her uncle had really been killed? And yet Gracie couldn't just leave her here standing on the corner in the wind. It would be dark very soon. It was after three already, and going to rain.

'Yer got a ma?' she asked.

'No,' Minnie Maude answered. 'I got an aunt Bertha, but she says as Charlie don't matter. Donkeys is donkeys.'

'Well, if yer uncle got killed, maybe she don't care that much about donkeys right now.' Gracie tried to sound reasonable. 'Wot's gonna 'appen to 'er, with 'im gone? Yer gotta think as she might be scared, an' all.'

Minnie Maude blinked. 'Uncle Alf didn't matter to 'er like that,' she explained. ''E were me pa's brother.' She sniffed harder. 'Uncle Alf told good stories. 'E'd been ter places, an' 'e saw things better than most folk. Saw them fer real, wot they meant inside, not just wot's plain. 'E used ter make me laugh.'

Gracie felt a sudden, sharp sense of the child's loss. Maybe it was Uncle Alf she was really looking for, and Charlie was just an excuse, a kind of sideways way of seeing it, until she could bear to look at it straight. There was something very special about people who made you laugh. 'I'm sorry,' she said gently. It had been a little while before she had really said to herself that her mother wasn't ever coming back.

''E were killed,' Minnie Maude repeated. 'Yesterday.'

'Then yer'd best go 'ome,' Gracie pointed out. 'Yer aunt'll be wondering wot's 'appened to yer. Maybe Charlie's already got 'ome 'isself.'

Minnie Maude looked miserable and defiant, shivering in the wind and almost at the end of her strength. 'No 'e won't. If 'e knew 'ow ter come 'ome 'e'd 'a been there last night. 'E's cold an' scared, an' all by 'isself. An' no one but 'im an' me knows as Uncle Alf were done in. Aunt Bertha says as 'e fell off an' 'it 'is 'ead, broke 'is neck most like. An' Stan says it don't matter anyway, 'cos dead is dead just the same, an' we gotta bury 'im decent, an' get on with things. Ain't no time ter sit around. Stan drives an 'ansom, 'e goes all over the place, but 'e don't know as much as Uncle Alf did. 'E could fall over summink without seeing it proper. 'E sees wot it is, like, Uncle Alf said, but 'e don't never see wot it could be! 'E didn't see as donkeys can be as good as a proper 'orse.'

Not for a hansom cab, Gracie thought. Whoever saw a hansom with a donkey in the shafts? But she didn't say so.

'An' Aunt Bertha didn't 'old with animals,' Minnie Maude finished. 'Except cats, 'cos they get the mice.' She gulped and wiped her nose on her sleeve again. 'So will yer 'elp me look for Charlie, please?'

Gracie felt useless. Why couldn't she have come a little earlier, when her gran first told her to? Then she wouldn't even have been here for this child to ask her for something completely impossible. She felt sad and guilty, but there was no possible way she could go off around the wet winter streets in thc dark, looking for donkeys. She had to get home with the vegetables so her gran could make supper for them, and the two hungry little boys her son had left when he died. They were nearly old enough to get out and earn their own way, but right now they were still a considerable responsibility, especially with Gran earning what she could doing laundry every hour she was awake, and a few when she hardly was. Gracie helped with errands; she always seemed to be running around fetching or carrying something, cleaning, sweeping, scrubbing. But very soon, when Spike and Finn didn't need watching, she would have to go to the factory like other girls.

'I can't,' she said quietly. 'I gotta go 'ome with the taters, or them kids'll start eating the chairs. Then I gotta 'elp me gran.' She wanted to apologise, but what was the point? The answer was still no.

Minnie Maude nodded, her mouth tightening a little. She breathed in and out deeply, steadying herself. ''S all right, I'll look fer Charlie meself.' She sniffed and turned away to walk home. The sky was darkening and the first spots of rain were heavy in the wind, hard and cold.

When Gracie pushed the back door open to their two-room lodgings in Heneage Street her grandmother was standing with a basin of water ready to wash and peel the potatoes. She looked worn out from spending all day up to her elbows in hot water, caustic and lye, heaving other people's wet linen from one sink to another, shoulders aching, back so sore she could hardly touch it. Then she would have to lift it all again to wind it through the mangles, which would squeeze the water out so that there would be some chance of getting it dry so it could be returned, and paid for. There was always need for money: rent, food, boots, a few sticks and a little coal to put on the fire, and of course Christmas.

Gracie hardly grew out of anything. It seemed as if she had stopped at four foot eleven, and worn-out pieces could always be patched. But Spike and Finn were bigger every time you looked at them – and considering how much they ate perhaps no one should be surprised.

The food was good, and every scrap disappeared, even though they were being careful and saving any treats for Christmas. Spike and Finn bickered a bit, as usual, then went off to bed obediently enough at about seven. There wasn't a clock, but if you thought about it, and you were used to the sounds of the street outside, footsteps coming and going, the voices of those you knew, then you had a good idea of time.

Having the two rooms wasn't bad, considering. There was the kitchen, with a tin bowl for washing in, the stove to cook and keep warm by, and the table and three chairs and a stool. And there was the bench for chopping, ironing, baking now and then. There was a drain outside the back door, a well at the end of the street, and a privy at the bottom of the yard. There was one other small room where Gracie and her gran had beds on one side, and on the other they had built a sort of bed for the boys. They lay in it, one at each end.

But Gracie did not sleep well that night, in spite of being very nearly warm enough. She could not forget Minnie Maude Mudway, standing on the street corner in the dusk, grieving for loneliness, death, a donkey who might or might not be lost. All night it troubled her, and she woke to the bleak, icy morning still miserable.

She got up quickly, without disturbing her gran, who needed every moment of sleep she could find. Gracie pulled on her clothes immediately; the air was as cold as stone on her skin. There was ice on the inside of the windows as well as the outside.

She tiptoed out into the kitchen, put on her boots and buttoned them up, then started to rake out the dead ashes from the kitchen stove and relight it so she could heat a pan of water, and make porridge for breakfast. That was a luxury not everyone had, and she tasted it with pleasure every time.

Spike and Finn came in before daylight, although there was a paling of the sky above the rooftops. They were full of good spirits, planning mischief, and glad enough to eat anything they were given: porridge, a heel of bread and a smear of dripping. By half-past eight they were off on errands for the woman at the corner shop, and Gran, fortified by a cup of tea, insisting it was enough, went on her way back to the laundry.

Gracie busied herself with housework, washing dishes, sweeping and dusting, putting out slops and fetching more water from the well at the end of the street. It was cold outside, a rime of ice on the cobbles and a hard, east wind promising sleet.

By nine o'clock she could not bear her conscience any more. She put on her heaviest shawl, grey-brown cloth and very thick, and went outside into the street and down to the corner to look for Minnie Maude.

London was an enormous cluster of villages all running into each other, some rich, some poor, none worse than Flower and Dean Street, which was filled with rotting tenements, sometimes eight or ten people to a room. It was full of prostitutes, thieves, magsmen, cracksmen, starglazers, snotter-haulers and fogle-hunters, pickpockets of every kind.

Oddly enough the boundaries remained. Each had its own identity and loyalty, its hierarchy of importance and rules of behaviour, its racial and religious mixtures. Just the other side of Commercial Street it was Jewish, mostly Russians and Poles. In the other direction was Whitechapel. Thrawl Street, where Minnie Maude said she lived, was beyond Gracie's area. Only something as ignorant as a donkey would wander regardless from one to another as if there were no barriers, just because you could not see them. Charlie could hardly be blamed, poor creature, but Minnie Maude knew, and of course Gracie did even more so.

At the corner the wind was harder. It sliced down the open street, whining in the eaves of the taller buildings, brick defaced with age, weathering and neglect. Water stains from broken guttering streaked black, and she knew these places would smell of mould inside, like dirty socks.

The soles of her boots slipped on the ice and her feet were so cold she could not feel her toes any more.

The next street over was busy with people, men going to work at the lumber yard or the coal merchant, girls going to the match factory a little further up. One passed her, and Gracie saw for a moment the lop-sided disfigurement of her face known as 'phossie-jaw', from the phosphorus in the match-heads. An old woman was bent over, carrying a bundle of laundry. Two others shared a joke, laughing loudly. There was a pedlar on the opposite corner with a tray of sand-wiches, and a man in a voluminous coat slouched by.

A brewer's dray passed, horses lifting their great feet proudly, clattering on the stones, harnesses gleaming even in this washed-out winter light. Nothing more beautiful than a horse, strong and gentle, its huge feet with hair like silk skirts around them.

A costermonger came a few yards behind, pushing a barrowful of vegetables, pearly buttons on his coat. He was whistling a tune, and Gracie recognised it as a Christmas carol – the words were something about merry gentlemen.

She walked quickly to get out of the wind; it would be more sheltered once she was round the corner. She knew what street she was looking for. She could remember the name, but she could not read the signs. She was going to have to ask someone, and she hated that. It took away all her independence and made her feel foolish. At least someone would know Minnie Maude, especially since there had just been a death in the family.

She was regarded with some suspicion, but five minutes later she stood on the narrow pavement outside a grimy, brick-fronted house whose colourless wooden door was shut fast against the ice-laden wind.

Until this moment Gracie had not thought of what she was going to say to explain her presence. She could hardly tell them that she had come to help Minnie Maude find Charlie, because if she were really a good person, she could have offered to do that yesterday. Going home to tea sounded like such an excuse. And anyway, Aunt Bertha had already said that, as far as she was concerned, it didn't matter and, whatever Minnie Maude thought of it, that seemed reasonable enough. The poor woman was bereaved, and probably beside herself with worry as to how they were going to manage without a money-earning member of the family. There would be a funeral to pay for, never mind looking for a daft donkey that had wandered off. Except that he might be worth a few shillings if they sold him.

Probably they already had, and just didn't want to tell Minnie Maude. She was too young to understand some of the realities of life. That was probably it. Better to, though. Then she would stop worrying that he was lost and scared and out in the rain by himself.

Gracie was still standing uselessly on the cobbles, shifting from one foot to the other and shaking with cold, when the door opened and a large man with a barrel chest and bow legs came out, banging his hands together as if they were already numb.

'Eh, mister!' Gracie stepped forward into his path. 'Is this where Minnie Maude lives?'

He looked startled. 'I ain't seen you 'ere before! Who are yer?' he demanded.

'I ain't been 'ere before,' Gracie said reasonably. 'That's 'ow I dunno if this is where she lives.'

He looked her up and down, all four foot eleven inches of her, from the top of her shawl, her pale, clever little face, down her bony body to her worn-out boots with buttons missing. 'Wot d'yer want with our Minnie Maude, then?' he asked suspiciously.

Gracie said the first thing that came into her mind. 'Got an errand for 'er. Worth tuppence, if she does it right. Can't do it all meself,' she added, in case it sounded too good to be true.

'I'll get 'er for yer,' the man said instantly, turning on his heel and going back into the house. A moment later he returned with Minnie Maude behind him. 'There y'are.' He pushed her forward. 'Make yerself useful then,' he prompted, as if she might be reluctant.

Minnie Maude's wide eyes regarded Gracie with wonder and gratitude entirely inappropriate to the offer of a tuppenny job, which might even last all day. Still, perhaps when you were eight, tuppence was a lot. Gracie was thirteen, and it was more than she actually had, but she had needed to make the offer good in order to be certain it would be carried inside, and Minnie Maude allowed to accept. She would deal with finding the tuppence later.

'Well, come on then!' she said aloud, grasping Minnie Maude's arm and half pulling her away from the bow-legged man, then striding along the street as fast as she dared on the ice.

'Yer gonna 'elp me find Charlie?' Minnie Maude asked breathlessly, struggling and slipping to keep up with her.

It was a little too late to justify her answer now. 'Yeah,' Gracie conceded. 'I expect it won't take long. Somebody'll 'ave seen 'im. Maybe 'e got a fright an' ran off. 'E'll get 'isself 'ome by an' by. Wot 'appened ter yer uncle Alf anyway?' She slowed down a little bit now they were round the corner and back in Brick Lane.

'Dunno,' Minnie Maude said unhappily. 'They found 'im in Richard Street, in Mile End, lying in the road with the back of 'is 'ead stove in, an' cuts an' bangs all over 'im. They said as 'e must 'ave fell off 'is cart. But Charlie'd never 'ave gone an' left 'im like that. Couldn't 'ave, even if 'e'd wanted to, bein' as 'e were tied inter the shafts.'

'Where's the cart, then?' Gracie asked practically.

'That's it!' Minnie Maude exclaimed, stopping abruptly. 'It's not there! That's 'ow else I know 'e were done in. It's gone.'

Gracie shook her head, stopping beside her. 'Who'd 'a done 'im in? Wot's in the cart, then? Milk? Coal? Taters?' She was beginning to feel more and more as if Minnie Maude were in her own world of loss and grief more than in the real one. 'Who's gonna do in someone fer a cartload of taters? 'E must 'a died natural, an' fell off, poor thing, then some rotten bastard stole 'is cart, taters an' all, an' Charlie with 'em. But 'owever rotten they are,' she added hastily, 'they'll look after Charlie, because 'e's worth summink. Donkeys are useful.'

'It weren't milk,' Minnie Maude said, easing her pace to keep in step. ''E were a rag-an'-bone man, an' sometimes 'e 'ad real beautiful things – treasures. It could 'a been anything.' She left the possibilities dangling in the air.

Gracie looked sideways at her. Minnie Maude was about three inches shorter than Gracie, and just as thin. Her small face had a dusting of freckles across the nose, and at the moment it was pinched with worry. Gracie felt a strong stab of pity for her.

''E'll maybe come back by 'isself,' she said as encouragingly as she could. 'Unless 'e's in a nice stable somewhere, an' can't get out. I expect someone nicked the cart 'cos there were some good stuff in it. But donkeys ain't daft.' She had never actually known a donkey, but she knew the coalman's horse, and it was intelligent enough. It could always find a carrot top, whatever pocket you put it in.

Minnie Maude forced a smile. 'Course,' she said bravely. 'We just gotta ask, before 'e gets so lost an' can't find 'is way back. Actually, I dunno 'ow far 'e's ever been. More'n I 'ave, probably.'

'Well, we'd best get started, then,' Gracie surrendered her common sense to a moment's weakness of sympathy. Minnie Maude was a stubborn little article, and daft as a brush with it. Who knew what would happen to her if she was left on her own? Gracie would give it an hour or two; she could spare that much. Maybe Charlie would come back himself by then.

'Thank yer,' Minnie Maude acknowledged. 'Where we gonna start?' She looked at Gracie hopefully.

Gracie's mind raced for an answer. 'Who found yer uncle Alf, then?'

'Jimmy Quick,' Minnie Maude replied immediately. ''E's a lying git, an' all, but that's probably true, 'cos 'e 'ad ter get 'elp.'

'Then we'll go an' find Jimmy Quick an' ask 'im,' Gracie said firmly. 'If 'e tells us exact, maybe takes us there, we can ask folks, an' perraps someone saw Charlie. Where'd we look fer 'im?'

'In the street.' Minnie Maude squinted up at the leaden winter sky, apparently judging the time. 'Maybe Church Lane, by now. Or maybe 'e ain't started yet, an' 'e's still at 'ome in Angel Alley.'

'Started wot?'

''Is way round. 'E's a rag-an'-bone man too. That's 'ow come 'e found Uncle Alf.'

'Rag-an'-bone men don't do the same round as each other,' Gracie pointed out. 'It don't make no sense. There'd be nuffink left.' She was as patient as she could be. Minnie Maude was only young, but she should have been able to work that out.

'I told yer 'e were a lying git,' Minnie Maude replied, unperturbed.

'Well, we'd better find 'im anyway.' Gracie had no better idea. 'Which way'd we go?'

'That way,' Minnie Maude pointed after a minute's hesitation in which she swivelled around slowly, facing each direction in turn. She set off confidently, marching across the cobbles, her feet clattering on the ice, and, with her heart in her mouth, Gracie caught up with her, hoping to heaven that they would not both get as lost as Charlie.

A Christmas Beginning

Anne Perry

For Superintendent Runcorn, Christmas has rarely looked so bleak. Believing that a change of scenery may help him finally forget Melisande Ewart, Runcorn heads for the beautiful, desolate Isle of Anglesey. Any hopes of Christmas passing quietly are dashed, however, when he discovers Melisande is also in Anglesey and, moreover, that she is engaged to another man.

Then the local vicar's sister is found murdered and Melisande's brother is implicated in the crime. Determined to assist Melisande in her time of need, Runcorn resolves to find the killer. Is it possible that, in doing so, he will also win the heart of his one true love?

A Christmas Beginning – a charming tale of love and hope played out against a background of deceit and death – is sure to warm your heart this holiday season.

Praise for Anne Perry's Christmas novellas:

'If Christmas puts you in the mood for a good Agatha Christie, try Perry' *Glasgow Evening Times*

'A bite-sized mystery that could be fitted in after your Christmas lunch' *Daily Telegraph*

978 0 7553 3431 5

headline

A Christmas Secret

Anne Perry

December 1890. Eleven days before Christmas, Clarice and her husband, Reverend Dominic Corde, arrive in the idyllic village of Cottisham to watch over the Reverend Wynter's flock whilst he takes a richly deserved holiday.

With its village green and thatched cottages, Cottisham is a far cry from the bleak London parish they've left behind. But Clarice can't shake the feeling that the welcoming smiles of the locals are hiding dark secrets.

When a shocking discovery confirms her suspicions, Clarice can't resist investigating. Could it be that the Reverend is not all that he seems? Are there black sheep in the fold? One thing is certain: Clarice is determined to uncover the truth. Even if it means putting her own life in danger.

A Christmas Secret – find the true meaning of Christmas in this spellbinding story of faith, hope and intrigue.

Acclaim for Anne Perry's novels:

'Delightful . . . The perfect gift for a whodunit addict who likes to curl up with a good book after Christmas lunch' *Oxford Times*

'The author has the eyes of a hawk for character nuance and her claws out for signs of . . . criminal injustice' *New York Times*

978 0 7553 3429 2

headline